It was a fire now. Inside her; burning her. Searing her belly. The Halston blouse was wet, the pale coffee colour black beneath her arms and across her breasts. Her nipples, not constrained by a brassiere, were hard, erected against the silk that seemed to chafe against them. They burned with a cold, tingling ache, as sometimes they did after a bout of vigorous sex. She cried out as the pain in her belly got worse, forcing the bile, burning and bitter, up her throat so that she choked on it. Her tensed arms began to shake and she was dimly aware of her teeth chattering. A castanet sound that sent prickling stabs up through her gums, into her sinuses, a counterpoint to the roaring of the agonizing red waves cascading through her insides. Around the wheel, her nails dug against her palms, hard enough to draw blood that she didn't notice. Tears flowed helplessly, blinding her as her foot, jerked now by the uncontrolled shuddering of her whole body, stamped harder against the accelerator.

My God, she thought.

It was the last clear thought she had . . .

STUART KINDER

The Institute

PANTHER
Granada Publishing

Panther Books
Granada Publishing Ltd
8 Grafton Street, London W1X 3LA

Published by Panther Books 1984

Copyright © Stuart Kinder 1984

ISBN 0-586-05931-8   68478422

Printed and bound in Great Britain by
Collins, Glasgow

Set in Times

My thanks are due to Nick Austin, whose fertile mind spawned shivers in the imagination.
To Jim Miles, who had an idea that changed the shape.
And to George A. Romero and David Cronenberg, without whose work this might never have happened.

1

The woman's hands were moist with perspiration as they gripped the leather-bound wheel of the matt black Porsche Carrera. She glanced at the unwinking red eye of the stop light, then reached across to fetch a Kleenex from the box on the passenger seat, crushing the tissue between her palms as a fresh wave of nausea hollowed her cheeks and beaded her forehead with sweat. She rolled the used tissue into a tight ball and dropped it carelessly on the carpeted floor as the light changed. Her hands were trembling slightly. Behind her a big Chevrolet let loose a horn blast that seemed to echo inside the confines of the smaller vehicle, and she winced as the sound aggravated the headache that was gnawing around the edges of her concentration. The Chevrolet honked a second time, and in her rear-view mirror she caught a glimpse of a fleshy, irritable face, lips moving to form unheard obscenities.

She put her left hand back on the wheel and shifted the gear stick forwards. Depressed the accelerator as she eased her foot from the clutch. The Porsche lurched, engine roaring as she pulled away from the noisy Chevrolet, shaking her head at the muffed gear change.

She reached the next intersection and halted for the red light, tugging a second Kleenex from the box to dab meticulously at her face. She checked her make-up in the mirror with the automatic precision of a woman with both the time and the money to take a great deal of care with her appearance. She didn't, she decided, look too bad. A little pale, maybe. A fraction the wrong side of fashionable slimness, the faint shadows beneath her eyes and cheekbones hinting at gauntness. But not too bad. In fact, not bad at all. Her hair, cut and high-lighted only yesterday in Nieman's, looked expensively casual. The Halston blouse and the St Laurent skirt did a lot for her complexion, and as yet there were no discernible signs of her waistline thickening or breasts filling out beyond their usual size. Maybe it was just nerves that made her feel sick. They'd told her that she wouldn't start to show much until the fifth or sixth month; that the exercise routines and regular medical checks, allied with the dietary supplements they had recommended, would keep her healthy as ever.

So why did she feel so damn' sick?

The Chevrolet sounded its horn again, the blast ringing right inside her skull this time so that she reacted with uncharacteristic irritation, stamping her foot hard against the gas pedal to send the Porsche forwards with a protesting squeal of scorched rubber. The needle of the rev. counter spun around the dial and she stamped on the brake as sun glinted bright from the polished chrome fender of the CanAm in front. The Porsche halted abruptly, throwing her forwards against the constraint of the safety belt. The material cut into her stomach, sending the nausea climbing like a column of scalding water into her throat. Her eyes watered, and for a moment she thought she would vomit. Blinking, she snapped the direction indicator over and turned to the side of the roadway, pulling clear of the traffic flow to allow the impatient Chevrolet past.

She leaned her head back against the smooth leather of the head restraint and gulped in lungsful of air. The sun was hot and bright on the tinted glass of the windows, but she could hear the faint purr of the air conditioning, and when she put a hand close to a vent the air was cool, almost chilly. Yet she could now feel moisture, slightly tacky, at her armpits and across her shoulders. And there was an uncomfortable, slightly chafing, dampness between her thighs. She pressed a tissue to her face, not bothering now about her make-up, and closed her eyes tight, trying to force the dizziness away. After a while it abated and she opened her eyes again. She reached up to adjust the mirror, then fetched mascara and a brush from the Gucci purse on the seat beside her. Deftly, she repaired the damage to her face. Eyes, lips, a dab of colour to her cheeks: a ritual carried out with expertise. She put her hands back on the wheel, automatically checking her nails. She glanced at the digital clock mounted to the right of the facia, seeing that she would be late for her appointment.

Too bad, she thought. Alice would have to wait a little. After all, pregnant women were surely entitled to a little leeway.

Then she thought, what the hell am I thinking about? Alice doesn't know yet. No one knows, except Larry and me. And the Institute, of course.

They had discussed – she and Larry – whether or not they should tell their friends, and decided against it. Time enough when she began to show the telltale signs of pregnancy. After seven years of childless marriage their friends had adopted a tactful silence, assuming they were a career-oriented couple. And to a large extent they were. Larry was heading for big things at the agency; a Vice Presidency, if the hints old Doug Cannon had been dropping at the last dinner party were true. And Kleinmann had been making noises about promoting her to chief designer. That could be fun: they didn't need the money, but it would be useful with a child on the way.

A child.

A baby.

Their baby.

He – she was confident it would be a boy – would be named Robert Laurence Anders. Robert for her father's sake, Laurence after Larry. If the Institute was wrong and it turned out to be a girl – though she knew it wouldn't – she would be called Sarah Louise, after her and Larry's mothers. They had spent a great deal of time discussing the names. Almost as much as they had spent making the original decision to approach the Institute. And even then it had been more complicated than she had expected. There had been lengthy interviews, medical check-ups, even psychiatric tests that had reminded her of college IQ gradings. The Institute had insisted on a financial review that Larry accepted only with reluctance, his desire for a child overcoming his desire to keep at least some part of their life private. And God knew, they charged enough. She and Larry had gone along with the formalities because the grapevine said the Institute was the best. The only one, really. And discreet, which was what they wanted. After all, who liked to admit the child she was bearing was the product of a test tube? That her womb was artificially fertilized? Two weeks in Oregon – explained to their friends as a vacation on a health farm – and then two more (a trip to Europe) for the actual business. She hated the medical word for it: it was too cold, too impersonal.

But it had all gone smoothly enough, and now the baby was there. Inside her.

Growing.

She put her make-up things back in the Gucci purse and opened the clear plastic phial they had given her. No more than four of the capsules a day, they had said, and already she had swallowed two. One in the bathroom when she felt certain she was about to throw up what little breakfast she had eaten and then a second as she dressed for her date with Alice. Perhaps she should hold the remainder for later: one for the evening, and the final gelatine ovoid to guarantee a decent night's sleep. Then her stomach sent a fresh message up to her brain and she palmed the capsule into her mouth. Without it, she was liable to make a fool of herself in the restaurant. Anyway, they always allowed a wide safety margin on painkillers. Or whatever it was the capsules contained.

She gagged slightly, forcing the thing down her dry throat. Then adjusted the air conditioning controls to a cooler output. Come on, she told herself, pull yourself together. You're healthy; you've got the best medical attention money can buy; you're a mother-to-be. You should be blooming. A few glasses of wine and a slice of that quiche Antonio makes so well. The kind of brittle, elegant conversation that was Alice's speciality. That'll make you feel better.

She glanced at the clock again. It was already seven after twelve and it would take a good thirty minutes to work her way through the noonday traffic. Ten more to park the car and walk the short distance to Lamar and Ross. She would definitely be late, unless she could make up some time.

She turned the mirror back in place, checked her side mirror, and pulled back into the traffic flow. The next section was devoid of lights and she eased into the fast lane, gunning the Porsche to a speed slightly above the legal fifty. When she hit the next stop light the nausea came back. She decided the capsule hadn't had time to work and tried not to think about the pain. The light changed and she started off again. The capsule would take effect soon: they always did, though the last few days the pleasantly numbing, slightly euphoric feeling they gave her hadn't seemed to last quite so long. She pressed a manicured finger against the *on* button of the pre-tuned Blaupunkt stereo system, hoping the music throbbing from the four speakers would drown out the throbbing inside her. She didn't usually drive with music playing, preferring to concentrate on handling the car. She was a good driver. Confidently fast, with a clean record. That was one reason Larry had bought her the Porsche, a combination of birthday gift and celebratory present. Maybe a chauffeur would have been better, the way she was feeling right now.

She pulled around a Buick as Willy Nelson told her his heroes had always been cowboys and the speedometer needle climbed steadily around the dial. She blinked some

11

more, running the tip of her tongue delicately over her dry lips. The turn-off came up soon. Just a few more minutes, then ease across to catch the down ramp for city centre. Yes: now. She checked her mirrors and began to change lanes, all her concentration focused on manoeuvring the Porsche towards the exit. Willy Nelson tailed off and the dj started to extol the virtues of someone's used car lot as she slowed for the turn. John Stewart came on, singing *Wheels of Thunder* as she made the turn, the blunt nose of the Porsche dipping as the ramp began.

She negotiated the first bend in the spiralling descent to the lower level as the music reached a crescendo that seemed to orchestrate the spasms hitting her. She punched the *off* button, killing the Blaupunkt, then whimpered as the slight forwards movement sent a fierce lance of pain stabbing through her insides. This was worse than it had ever been. The damned capsule wasn't doing anything for her and there was no place she could halt the car. Not until she was off the ramp and clear of the cloverleaf below. She recalled a service station just beyond the cloverleaf. She would stop there: use the powder room. This time she was definitely going to throw up. Alice would just have to wait.

She looked at the clock. It said 12.16.

She didn't notice the speedometer or the rev. counter.

She was only aware of the pain swelling inside her and the dull, throbbing ferocity inside her head.

The Porsche gathered speed as the ramp angled more steeply, the suspension dipping to the side as the black car hit the curves. Her knuckles blanched as she clutched the wheel, and she bit her lower lip, groaning now, tears spilling from her eyes. The tail swung wide, the rear fender thumping against the low metal guard rail so that she over-corrected, veering off to the far side. She swung the wheel back into line, not lifting her foot from the gas pedal in her urgency to reach the service station before the pain got too fierce.

12

It was a fire now. Inside her; burning her. Searing her belly and filling her throat and mouth with the sour taste of bile. The Halston blouse was wet, the pale coffee colour black beneath her arms and across her breasts. Her nipples, not constrained by a brassiere, were hard, erected against the silk that seemed to chafe against them. They burned with a cold, tingling ache, as sometimes they did after a bout of vigorous sex. She cried out as the pain in her belly got worse, forcing the bile, burning and bitter, up her throat so that she choked on it and opened her mouth to spit it heedlessly down the cleavage of her blouse. Her tensed arms began to shake and she was dimly aware of her teeth chattering. A castanet sound that sent prickling stabs up through her gums, into her sinuses, a counterpoint to the roaring of the agonizing red waves cascading through her insides. Around the wheel, her nails dug against her palms, hard enough to draw blood that she didn't notice. Tears flowed helplessly, blinding her as her foot, jerked now by the uncontrollable shuddering of her whole body, stamped harder against the accelerator.

My God, she thought, *I'm going to wet myself*.

It was the last clear thought she had.

Patrolman David Koch heard the car before he saw it. From the tyre squeal alone he recognized a speeder, then the rasp of metal on metal told him he had a runaway. Three years riding Highway Patrol had taught him to analyse such sounds with something approaching ninety percent accuracy.

He swung onto the saddle of the big Harley Davidson and gunned the bike to snarling, authoritative life. As he pulled out from the overhang the flashers mounted across the bars crimsoned into warning iridescence and the siren began its uneven wailing. He was weaving through the traffic as the Porsche hit the cloverleaf, his eyes cold behind the dark glasses.

.The black car came off the ramp at a speed Koch calculated was close to sixty miles an hour. It veered across the lane markers, clipping the nose of a Ford so that the sedan spun into a Cadillac, driving the larger automobile off course into the path of a truck. Koch winced as a battery of lights came on across the tail of the big Mack and the airhorn screamed a useless warning. Then he mouthed a curse as the sixteen wheels locked and the Mack slid inexorably into the Cadillac. The Porsche went on moving, slowed only slightly by the impact. It crossed four lanes of road, careening off a Buick with a terrific clatter of rending metal. A Mustang, fish-tailing in a desperate attempt to avoid a nose-to-tail pile up, clipped the rear of the Porsche, sending the German car into a whirligig spin that bounced it over the kerb. It took a sign down, then demolished a row of ornamental bushes as the rear wheels gained traction and hurled the sports car back across the highway. A Volkswagen lost its offside front wing as the Porsche hit it, and then the runaway slammed into the barrier guarding the central reservation, crumpling the metal along with its own black bodywork. The wheels went on spinning as though the German car was trying to grind its way through the barrier, then stopped as the engine cut out and gasoline began to leak from the ruptured tank.

Koch steered his bike past the multi-vehicle pile-up. The flow had been moving slow enough that there was little chance of serious injury, and already most of the drivers were examining the damage, turning to stare at the big Harley as it closed in on the Porsche. Koch had the microphone of his radio up close to his mouth, sending in a request for assistance, ambulances, and a wreck crew. He halted the bike as he gave the location to the despatcher and dismounted with his right hand flipping the safety strap clear of the Magnum .357 holstered on his hip.

He kept his hand on the cross-hatched grips of the gun as he approached the stalled Porsche. The interior was

14

hidden behind the tinted glass and he could not tell how many occupants the car held. Nor what condition they were in. He wondered if the driver was drunk, or high on something. He felt angry: he didn't like stupid accidents. Nor did he like crazy drivers. Or expensive foreign cars. Or having his lunch delayed by some goddam lunatic with more money to waste on imported sports jobs than he could hope to make in months of riding herd on their goddam crazy antics.

He dragged the Magnum clear of the holster as he paced up behind the wrecked Porsche.

There was no movement inside so far as he could tell, so he shouted for the driver to step out. There was still no movement, nor any answer, and he eased up a little closer with the Magnum stuck out in front ready to use. He got alongside the car and tapped on the glass. When nothing happened, he grabbed the handle and swung the door open.

Then he said, 'Jesus!', and stood there with his mouth hanging wide and the pistol forgotten in his hand.

The Porsche hadn't picked up so many hits that the impact would have killed the driver, but the woman belted in behind the leather-wrapped wheel was as dead as anyone Koch had seen. She was – had been – a good-looker. Expensively dressed, in keeping with the car. Koch noticed all that with professional objectivity. He noticed that her eyes were blue and opened wide enough that white showed all around the pupils. Her mouth, too, was opened wide enough he could see down her throat, the lips drawn back off very white teeth that indicated either a healthy life, or some pricey dental work. The teeth were bared as though the woman had been in a lot of pain. There was vomit on her lips and down the front of her blouse, yellow and sticky against the sweat-soaked darkness of the thin material. She had good tits: firm and nicely shaped. Her hands were still on the wheel, the fingers locked in place under intense pressure. There was blood on her wrists.

15

What shocked the patrolman, however, was the sheer amount of blood elsewhere. There was so much it was difficult to see where it came from. Her skirt was drenched, thick crimson pooling between her legs and soaking into the cloth of her skirt so that it was dragged down by the weight of the viscous liquid, riding up over her knees and outlining her thighs. She had good legs. It was on her abdomen, too; a tide line dark across her midriff as though the blood sought to climb up her body to meet the sticky traces of vomit. It was still oozing from her, driven by gravity to spread over the leather of the contoured seat in sufficient quantity that it spilled over the lip and was dripping turgidly onto the carpet covering the floor of the car.

Koch reached in to check the pulse he knew wouldn't be beating, then ran his gaze professionally over the corpse, looking for a wound, some sign of injury that would explain the amount of blood. There was nothing. No bullet hole to suggest a sniper's work, nor any sign of serious hurt from the impact of the collisions. The woman, protected by the safety harness and the deep, wrap-around seat, hadn't even picked up any bruises. From the way she was sitting and the rigidity of her arms, Koch knew she hadn't been thrown against the wheel hard enough to produce haemorrhaging. A haemorrhage of that cause would, anyway, have resulted in oral bleeding, and there was no sign of that. Just the blood coming from under her skirt.

It was thick, intestinal blood. Almost too thick, as though mixed with the fabric of her insides. It smelled thick; sweet and rich and cloying. The air conditioning – still running – did nothing to dispel the sickening odour and Koch slammed the door closed, breathing hard as he tried to recall where he had smelled blood like that before.

It came to him as he walked back to the Harley Davidson and lifted his incident report pad from the plastic clip-on. It had been about a year, maybe a year and a half, ago. On Interstate 45 between Ennis and Palmer. He had flagged down a speeding Lincoln convertible and got a shock when he found a heavily pregnant woman and her distraught husband inside. He had done his best to get them to an emergency centre in time, but not quite made it. One lousy half mile too soon the husband had started honking his horn and Koch had found himself struggling to remember his paramed training as the mother bawled and the baby came into the world on a fanfare of approaching sirens and the monotonous cursing of the sweating cop. That was where he had smelled blood like that before.

He said, 'Jesus!' again, this time thoughtfully, and listened to the sirens getting closer. He went over to the car and began to check out the licence. It didn't look like he was going to eat this shift, but that didn't seem to matter now: his appetite was gone.

The DPD was first on the scene with two bikemen and a blue-and-white. Then a paramed wagon and an ambulance emblazoned with the green and gold insignia of the Dallas Memorial Hospital. The patrolmen started in on the detail work and began to clear the highway while the medical team tended the few minor injuries incurred. Koch filled in his report form and stayed by the Porsche, interested in hearing what the medic from the hospital would say.

He was glad to see that the doctor riding with the ambulance crew was Mike Stoner. Stoner was an OK guy who knew his job and didn't go much for the red tape that took up too much of his and everyone else's time. He was too damn' good-looking – like a medic in a tv serial – but he was all right. Koch trusted him.

He gave the patrolman a tight grin as he ran from the ambulance with a new-looking black bag in his hand.

17

'Dave?' He was already opening the door of the Porsche. 'What we got?'

'One dead.' Koch took off his helmet and rubbed a hand over his close-cropped hair. 'Driver. Nothing else serious.'

Stoner whistled faintly when he saw the corpse and reached in to check the pulse.

'I done that already.' Koch noticed that the cuff of Stoner's white smock was smeared with blood. 'I think she was dead before she crashed.'

Stoner said nothing. He was checking the body with swift, impersonal efficiency. He didn't seem to notice the smell.

Finally he stood up and palmed the door closed again. He wiped his hands clean and pushed a lock of fair hair back from his forehead. He was frowning.

'Well?' Koch asked. 'What's the verdict?'

Stoner shrugged. 'Hard to say without an autopsy. It looks like severe haemorrhaging. Why, I don't know.'

'Drugs?' queried the patrolman. 'You see her eyes?'

'Maybe.' Stoner snapped his bag shut. 'The pupils are dilated, but that could be shock. Or fear. I don't know anything would make her bleed that much so fast. And still let her drive a car.'

'The smell,' said Koch. 'You notice the smell?'

'Hard not to.' Stoner grinned, not showing any humour on his tanned face. 'Like the Delivery Room.'

'Yeah.' Koch nodded. 'What I thought. You think she was pregnant?'

Stoner shrugged again. 'If she was, it was too early to show. No external signs. I guess we wait for the autopsy results.'

'Yeah.' Koch fastened his helmet back in place. 'I guess we do. Meanwhile, I got paperwork. See you round.'

Stoner nodded and turned to the waiting ambulance-men. 'All right, you can get her loaded. Take her direct to the morgue.'

18

Already the woman was becoming a statistic. Koch would file his accident report; Stoner his medical report. The next of kin would be traced and informed. The findings of the autopsy would go down in the records and the bureaucratic machinery of the city of Dallas would be satisfied. A Social Security number would be deleted; a medical insurance file marked *Closed*: *Deceased*. The woman would become one more of the city's dead. No longer a person: just a file reference.

Stoner watched as the ambulancemen sealed the body-bag and slung it onto a trolley. Christ! he thought, just like meat for the freezer. Just like watching the choppers loading back in 'Nam. He looked away to the car, admiring the sleek lines, scarred now and buckled by the crash. She had money, whoever she was. Those clothes cost plenty, the car plenty more.

He noticed a purse on the hood. Koch must have checked the contents, then forgotten it. Stoner picked it up, glancing at the entwined gold *Gs*, bright against the blood-stained leather: a Gucci number. Fay had one like it, that was how he recognized it and knew it cost. He laughed at himself for the faint twinge of resentment he felt: all right, the woman had been wealthy, that wasn't a crime. Any more than it was a crime Fay's people having money. Hell! he wore the Gucci belt she'd given him last Christmas, and she wore the one he'd given her for her birthday. She'd been pleased with it. Almost as pleased as she was with the set of matching Louis Vuiton luggage her parents had given her, together with a note heavy on hints about its practical use. Like on a honeymoon. Which her father would be more than happy to pay for.

Fay, he thought, you're one of the best things that ever happened to me. But I'm not ready for marriage just yet. Not until I can afford to give you the same kind of treatment your father doles out.

He was still holding the purse as he climbed into the ambulance and the big V8 motor growled into life. Idly curious, he snapped the clasp open and began to study the contents. Like the clothes and the car, they spelled money. There was a lot of make-up stuff that he ignored; a small spray bottle of St Laurent perfume; a cheque book with the stubs bearing some very expensive names and equally impressive amounts; a wallet heavy with credit cards; an ID card.

The dead woman had been 32 years old. Her name had been Marianne Anders. Her address had been an exclusive block of apartments in an exclusive residential section. The Porsche had been registered in her name.

Yeah, he thought, plenty of money.

Then he thought, What was a woman like that doing bleeding to death behind the wheel of a very expensive imported sports car? Dave Koch had been right about the Delivery Room smell – there was a distinct suggestion of womb fluids in the odour of the blood. And it couldn't have been drugs or poison, not any kind that he knew about. An abortion? No – it couldn't be. Ladies who lived in Hillcrest and drove Porsche sports cars didn't get that kind of abortion. They went away for a spell. To some discreet clinic where a great deal of money changed hands and no questions got asked. Hell, he'd arranged a couple of those himself. So: not a botched termination.

But there was still that damned smell. It was in his nostrils now, like a nagging memory that lurks around the edges of consciousness and refuses to either identify itself properly, or go away. It was intriguing him and irritating him in equal measure. He folded the ID back into the purse and began to sort through the personal papers.

There was a note from someone called Alice, written on expensive, heavy-grain paper (like Fay's family used) with an embossed crest at the top. It suggested meeting for lunch, and the date was today's. He wondered if Alice was waiting somewhere: she'd wait a long time. There were some cards. Dress shops and small, exclusive shoe stores, a lingerie boutique; there was a doctor's card that would make the autopsy a little easier if they could get her medical records. A few others, mostly visiting cards with addresses in the Dallas/Fort Worth area. And one more. Just a name and an out-of-state telephone number. He didn't recognize the code, and the tasteful lettering – dark brown on purest white – said simply, *The Walters Institute*. He dropped it back in the purse with the others and tossed the bag onto the seat as the ambulance pulled into the receival area of the Dallas Memorial Hospital.

2

Stoner watched the corpse wheeled away, invisible and impersonal in the dull plastic of the bodybag. It jarred with the reassuring brightness of the hospital: a bleak reminder that people died here too. He glanced up at the imposing frontage, all plate glass and tasteful stone. It had been designed by a Scandinavian – someone called Haakinen or Sorensen, he could never remember – and it had an air of quiet confidence that seemed to say, we can cure you here. He wasn't sure why he didn't like it; it was a fine hospital in an area that demanded the best, and it offered the best available service. But there was still something about the obvious opulence that grated on some puritanical nerve in his psychological make-up. Whatever, it was one whole lot better than working out of a wood and canvas hootch with VC mortars going off in counterpoint to the screaming of the wounded. Better than the ill-funded and ramshackle place he had served his early days in. He yawned, blinking in the bright afternoon sunshine, and went inside.

Beyond the wide, automatic doors the place was cool, the air faintly redolent of flowers and ozone. It was a sterile atmosphere, the entire building effectively a series of individual units, each one sealed against bacterial penetration by a combination of air-purifying units and connecting corridors that were the closest things to air-locks this side of a space shuttle. Canned music droned calmly (soporifically?) from discreet speakers, and the cushioned flooring effectively blanked out the clatter of heels. Stoner went over to the wide, white desk that looked directly onto the doors and grinned at the receptionist.

The girl smiled back. Like the dead woman, she had very white teeth, spaced evenly in a mouth that was wide and full-lipped. Her lips were a discreet red, complementing the auburn of her hair, which she wore a fraction longer than hospital standards liked. Stoner liked her for that.

He said, 'Hi, Jenny,' and pulled a report form towards him.

'Anything exciting?' she asked.

'DOA.' Stoner began to complete the form. 'Out near the Grand Avenue cloverleaf. Some kind of haemorrhage.'

Jenny took the form and stacked it in an upright file tray, time indexed, with colour coded sections. She cross-referenced the report with automatic precision, then turned back to Stoner. The smile was still on her face: he was, in her opinion, the best-looking doctor in the place, and she hoped she could score with him some day.

'You look bushed. Was it bad?'

'Messy.' He shrugged. 'I'm curious about it. Like to see the autopsy report when it comes through.'

'I'll let you know.' She leaned forwards to give him a better view of her cleavage. Like her hair, the unfastened buttons broke regulations. 'It shouldn't be long – we've been quiet, lately.'

'Thanks.' He smiled absently, thinking more about the dead woman than the live female in front of him. 'I'm going for coffee, anyone wants me.'

'Sure.' She made a note on the duty roster. 'See you.'

Stoner waved, crossing the reception area to one of the rubber-sheathed doors. He glanced at his watch as he paced down the corridor: 1.38. Time enough to grab a coffee and a sandwich and hope the remaining one hour and twenty-two minutes of his shift would pass quietly. Jenny had been right: he was bushed. He had come on duty at 2.30 that morning, after little more than two hours sleep, following a dinner party with Fay and some friends of hers she'd said were in horses, or oil. Stoner wasn't sure

23

which, because they'd bored him and he'd not bothered paying too much attention to the conversation, which as best he could recall had revolved around the latest series of Opec talks and the chances of a horse he'd never heard of winning a race he wasn't interested in.

He went into the cafeteria reserved for medical staff on standby and poured himself a coffee. Black, no sugar. The vending machine delivered a cheese and bologna sandwich that he carried over to a vacant table, exchanging greetings along the way. He broke the seal on the sandwich and tossed the cellophane wrapping into a nearby disposal unit, hoping that this time the food wouldn't taste of the plastic. He was disappointed.

He was halfway through the sandwich when Fay came in. She was wearing a dark blue silk blouse and matching slacks. There was a small plastic tag on the front of the blouse – which she wore buttoned according to the regulations – that read, *Fay Nicholas. Admin.* Her blonde hair was gathered up behind her head, emphasizing the clean lines of her face and the fullness of her mouth. Her clear blue eyes shone as she caught sight of him.

'Mike.' She bussed him briefly and sat down, sneaking a sip of his coffee. 'Jenny said I'd find you here.'

He smiled at her. Warmly. 'You look good. Considering.'

'Last night?' She chuckled, a deep, affectionate sound. 'I thought they'd never go.'

'They weren't the most exciting people I've met.' Stoner finished the sandwich and wiped crumbs from his hands.

'Friends of the family.' Fay shrugged. 'Daddy likes me to entertain them every so often.'

'Yeah.' Stoner sipped coffee. 'But not too often, huh?'

He had known Fay Nicholas for a little over a year now, since she joined the hospital's administrative staff. He had begun dating her almost immediately, attracted by her blonde good looks and her ready sense of humour. She was, in many ways, everything a man could want. She was attractive, intelligent, eager in bed. And she had money. Family money. George Nicholas had a great deal of money and he liked to see his only daughter got her share. Enough that she was independently wealthy. She had taken the admin. job because she wanted – she had told him – to prove to herself and to her parents that she could stand on her own feet. And she had done exactly that: she earned a living like any other girl, not touching the money her father put into her account. That was a powerful point in her favour, but Stoner couldn't forget that family background. George Nicholas wouldn't let him. Nor, to a lesser extent, would Fay. They had begun sleeping together a month after their first date, and now more or less lived together. She had kept on her apartment, but spent more time in Stoner's three rooms down town than in the luxurious split-level given her as a Twenty-First present. Her ambition was to see herself the wife of Michael Stoner, Consultant. For which lucrative opportunity he needed do only two things: marry Fay and accept George's gift of getting him started. The one thing, he had been thinking about; the other, he refused pointblank. Last night had been a reminder of the strings the Nicholas family were good-heartedly trying to attach to him.

Fay made a move, pretending irritation. 'You'd rather have had Rafe over, I suppose.'

'He's livelier,' grinned Stoner.

'By about one bottle,' Fay retorted. 'After that, he's out.'

She accepted his friendship with Rafe Antrim in much the same way Rafe had accepted her: warily. In her opinion, Rafe was a potentially bad influence on a young doctor destined – with Nicholas help – for higher things. He drank too much and she was afraid he might persuade Mike to go out and do the things he sometimes – usually after a heavy session with Rafe – threatened.

Like dispensing medicine where it really counted. Joining what tattered remnants of the old Peace Corps were left; things like that. In turn, Rafe looked with suspicion on Fay's background, considering her a middle-class tie holding Mike back from doing what he really wanted. They had worked out a kind of unspoken truce with Stoner in the middle, sometimes as contact point between them, sometimes as mediator. Neither had really sought Stoner's opinion, which was simply that right now he was doing exactly what he wanted. So why the fuss?

'Rafe's OK,' he said; realizing it was a reflex defence. Then changed the subject: 'When are you off?'

'Four,' she replied. 'You'll be home by then?'

He nodded. 'I'm getting some sleep.'

'I'll try not to disturb you.'

She chuckled again, one foot reaching out under the table to stroke over his ankle.

'I'm getting some sleep first,' he corrected.

'Then what?' She was smiling as she said it.

'We'll see.' He took her hand. 'I thought maybe the movies. After.'

She went on smiling as she disengaged her hand and stood up.

'See you later.'

He nodded, watching as she crossed the room, hips swaying with the kind of controlled grace that comes only with natural ability developed to a fine art in the very best of finishing schools. In Fay's case, somewhere in Switzerland. An Intern whistled, and Stoner grinned: the open admiration gave him a pleasantly proprietorial feeling. He finished his coffee and fetched a second cup over to the table, hoping his buzzer wouldn't sound before his shift finished.

It didn't, and at 3.00 he exchanged his white smock for a jacket and walked round to the big parking lot behind the hospital to fetch his Mustang. Thirty minutes later he was in the apartment, pouring Jack Daniels over ice cubes as he stared through the window at the heat haze decorating the city. He stripped as he finished the drink, then climbed into the shower. When Fay came in he was asleep.

Laurence Anders looked up from the marketing report he was reading when the intercom on his desk buzzed. A frown of irritation creased his face as he flicked the switch to *receive*: he had given instructions not to be disturbed.

His secretary said, 'It's the police, Larry. They say it's important.'

Her tone transformed the frown from irritation to apprehension and he noticed his palm was sweaty as he lifted the receiver.

Inside three minutes his face was pale, jaw hanging slack as he stared into the blank abyss of disbelief. The telephone, dropped unheeded onto the leather desktop, gave off a low whine. There was a tapping on his door that he didn't hear, then his secretary came in, her own face creasing in concern as she saw him. She went over to the imitation antique globe standing to one side of the room and poured whisky. He took the glass with a hand that she noticed was trembling and swallowed the liquor in a single gulp.

'It's Marianne.' His voice was a dull monotone. 'She's dead.'

The woman said, 'Oh my God!' and refilled his glass, pouring a smaller measure for herself.

Anders said, 'I'd better call the hospital.'

The woman put down her glass and dialled the number.

Michael Stoner stirred in his sleep, the void replaced with the beginnings of dream images, the images erotic. Beside him, Fay let her hand run down his chest, over the flat muscle of his stomach; lower. Stoner grunted and turned to face her. The images became more erotic as she pressed

27

against him, mingling with tactile reality so that he reached for her, still not awake, and began to nuzzle her full breasts. She sighed, guiding his hands. And Stoner let reality take the place of the dreaming.

It was dusk when he woke again, the sheets rumpled. He stretched lazily, aware that he was alone in the bed, then swung his legs clear and stood up. Naked, he went into the apartment's large living area. Fay was dressed in a black silk kimono, a headset plugged into the hi-fi equipment. Stoner kissed her on the cheek and cut the tape. She took off the earphones and smiled at him.

'All right, lover, it's after. What are we doing tonight?'

'Movies?' he suggested. 'There's a Louis Malle on.'

'Sounds good.' She stood up, the kimono swirling clear of long, tanned legs. Stoner caught a memory of the dream. Then cursed as the telephone shrilled.

Fay watched as he picked it up, his face losing the smile as he listened to the voice at the other end. Finally he said, 'Yeah. OK. I'll do it now.' She raised her eyebrows, parodying a question, and Stoner grimaced.

'That was Eddison.' Eddison was Assistant Administrator. 'Seems like the husband of that DOA wants to talk to the doctor who saw her.'

'Why?' Fay wandered over to the glass table where he kept his liquor and began to mix a martini. 'There's been no autopsy yet.'

'Money.' Stoner picked up the telephone again and began to dial. 'The husband is some kind of bigwig. Eddison's afraid he'll get upset.'

Fay shrugged, dropping an olive into the glass. She held it towards Stoner, who shook his head, then motioned for her to keep silent as he began to speak. Fay listened to his end of the conversation.

'Mister Anders? This is Doctor Stoner. Michael Stoner. I attended the scene of the crash . . . What? No. I don't think so. The police can tell you better, but I don't think so. It didn't look that way to me. No. Blood loss . . . Yes,

28

that's right. Before . . . I think that caused the crash . . . Autopsy? Of course, that's regulations. There has to be . . . No, not yet. A day or so. Sure. I'll let you know. Personally? OK. I'm sorry. Yeah. Yeah, that's right.'

'Problems?' Fay sipped her martini.

'Not really.' Stoner's face was thoughtful. 'He wanted to know if the crash killed her.'

'Did it?' Fay added an ice cube.

'No.' Stoner shook his head. 'I don't know what was the cause. She'd haemorrhaged. There was massive blood loss from the bowels, but I'm damned if I can think what might have caused it. I asked Jenny for the autopsy report.'

'Why?' Fay got a hands-off look at the mention of Jenny's name that made Stoner grin.

'Idle curiosity,' he murmured. 'I never saw anything like it before.'

He glanced at the digital clock on the front of his VCR and patted Fay's hip. 'Let's go. We'll miss the movie.'

Across town Laurence Anders sat at his desk. The blinds were pulled on the windows of his office and the building was quiet, save for the murmur of cleaning machines drifting faintly down the carpeted corridors, almost cut off by the thick doors. A single lamp shone from its wall mounting behind him, etching shadows on a face already haggard. A half empty bottle of imported Scotch stood on the desk, rings of moisture spoiling the expensive leather of the surface. Anders' eyes were hollow, but as he reached for the bottle his hand was steady. He topped his glass, then consulted a small, gold-edged address book before lifting the telephone again.

He dialled an Oregon number.

The movie to which Stoner took Fay was Louis Malle's *Atlantic City*. They had both seen it before, and enjoyed it enough to return again. The trouble was, Stoner knew it well enough by now that he didn't – or couldn't – concentrate on the action. He kept seeing Marianne Anders' face. And the blood pooling the seat of the Porsche. And he kept thinking he could smell that curious odour, like the redolence of the Delivery Room.

He remained abstracted throughout the evening, walking the block separating the cinema from the taco restaurant Fay had chosen with his head down and his mind a long way away. Fay let him think: she had seen him like this before, usually when he was talking about his experiences in Viet Nam, or discussing the ethics of commercialized medicine with Rafe Antrim. She knew better than to interrupt his train of thought. Knew it was best to leave him to work it out in his own time. He'd discuss it with her eventually.

They finished eating and walked back to Stoner's Mustang. He drove back to the apartment and parked the car in silence. Was still silent as they prepared for bed.

'Want to talk about it?' she asked as they climbed between the sheets.

He shook his head. 'Not yet. I need to work it out yet. OK?'

'Sure.' She put her arms around him. 'It can keep.'

He responded to her embrace, but as he kissed her he couldn't help seeing Marianne Anders' face again.

3

Chicago basked in an autumn heatwave. In the concrete canyons of the city the glare of the sun was reflected back off the plate glass and shining steel frontages to send the temperature climbing towards the hundred mark. What little breeze there was came in off Lake Michigan to remind the inhabitants of the pollution fouling the water, combining with the outpourings of factories and the exhaust fumes of the constant traffic so that an odour of heat and decay seemed to fill the streets. Heat prostration was already claiming victims, and the transition from air-conditioned interiors to the cauldron outside was accounting for an unusually high crop of minor ailments.

The woman dressing in an apartment overlooking Wolf Lake was not looking forward to going out into the heat. The apartment was cool, the air conditioning unit turned up to maximum and venetian blinds drawn over the windows. It was a large apartment, a long, wide living area with sliding doors opening onto a balcony decorated with exotic plants that seemed the only things thriving in the heat. There were two bedrooms, each large, and a spacious bathroom. The kitchen was of a size to contain an adequate dining area, equipped with a range of gadgets that might have come from the pages of *Vogue* or *Harpers*. The whole place spoke of money and taste. The woman fitted it as a hand might a tailored glove. She was in her early thirties, her figure trimmed by regular exercise, her appearance maintained by regular trips to beauticians, manicurists and expensive hairdressers. The care she lavished on her appearance created an impression of svelte, sophisticated allure that overcame her essentially plain features. She was, in many ways, a living monument to that archetypal American dream: success. She was independently wealthy, having inherited a considerable amount on the death of both her parents in a motor accident three years before. She had been divorced once – nine months ago – and received generous alimony from her ex-husband, who preferred to settle a regular amount on her, rather than argue his disgust at finding her in bed with the woman with whom she now lived.

She had a date for cocktails with Jean, after which they were going on to a dinner party that promised to be amusing enough to take her mind off the heat. Had she been able, she would have gone to Europe for a month or two, long enough anyway for this damned heat to abate. But Jean was a working girl, holding down a job in the Chicago office of News International, and she had refused pointblank to go away. The woman sighed, checking the small gold Tissot on her slender wrist before selecting a cream silk blouse from the walk-in wardrobe that covered one wall of the bedroom. She fastened the blouse and chose a matching skirt, not bothering with hose in this heat – she had, anyway, a good enough tan that she could dispense with stockings. She took a pair of Louis Jourdan shoes from the racks at the base of the wardrobe and carried them over to the bed. She sat down there and bent to fasten the ankle straps, then winced as her stomach complained at the movement. She ignored the sudden stab of pain as she buckled the straps, rubbing her flat midriff as she stood up. She went into the bathroom and took a small plastic phial from the cabinet there, dropping a gelatine capsule into her hand, then transferring it to her mouth. She swallowed dry, checking her hair and make-up as she wondered if she had made the right decision.

She had always wanted children, but her marriage had proven barren. Tests had shown that was Ed's fault, if it was anyone's *fault*, but he had never really accepted that. It had been one of the reasons for their divorce. That and her growing awareness of her sexual orientation, culminating in her seduction by Jean. After the divorce they had bought the apartment together and worked out a lifestyle that suited them both. The one thing it lacked was a child. They had spent a great deal of time, she and Jean, discussing that. Adoption had seemed unlikely, and – to her – somehow distasteful. It was irrational, but she couldn't help that – if she was to raise a child, then she wanted a product of her own body, but without – if possible – the natural assistance of a man. Jean had come up with the answer after discreet enquiries amongst their wide circle of friends. There was a place that might help, they had learned, if it would accept them. It had, after extensive interviews that established them both as of suitable social and economic background, of acceptable IQ and emotional stability. Not to mention the physical side. The extensive nature of the tests had surprised her – rather pleasantly as the exclusiveness of the place impressed itself on her. It had been expensive, but that was no problem, and she had gone ahead to sign the papers.

That had been seven months ago, and for four months now, she had been pregnant.

She turned automatically to check her waistline in the floor-to-ceiling mirror occupying one wall of the bathroom. Fine: she was showing nothing yet. No bulge – the one part she did not look forward to. In fact, there had been no real sign that she was pregnant at all beyond a touch of nausea occurring in the mornings. The heatwave seemed to have made that worse. It was as though the sullen brilliance of the sky stirred something inside her, and for the past couple of weeks the nausea had been more frequent and more powerful than before.

She shrugged it off, glancing again at the watch as she quit the bathroom and collected her Vuiton purse from the living area. She adjusted Yves St Laurent sunglasses over her eyes and knotted a Hermès scarf she had picked up in London last year around her neck. She looked good, she decided: cool, calm and confident. She went out of the apartment, checking the police lock before walking down the plushly carpeted corridor to the elevator.

On the first floor she greeted the uniformed doorman with a smile, nodding in answer to his query of a cab. She waited inside the cool lobby until the cab was called, then stepped out into the heat. It struck her forcibly. It was like stepping out into cloying soup, accentuating the twinge of nausea she had felt earlier so that she groaned softly as she ducked to climb inside the brilliant yellow vehicle.

The driver glanced in his mirror, ugly face creasing in an expression of concern as he saw her reflection.

'You all right, lady?' His voice was worried. 'You look kinda sick.'

She shook her head, mumbling something in reply, and the driver gunned the motor, shrugging as he pulled into the traffic flow.

She gave him instructions and he went north on Avenue O, heading for 106th Street. Inside the cab, the air was muggy. It smelled of cigarette smoke and body odour. She stared at the driver's broad shoulders, seeing beads of sweat on the folds of his neck, dark shadows under the armpits of his short-sleeved bowling shirt. The nausea was worse now, accentuated by the fetid air inside the cab. She swallowed hard, wondering if she should change her mind. Go back to the cool comfort of the apartment and call Jean to tell her the evening was off. She decided against it: Jean would be angry and the last thing she could face right now was an argument. Better to continue, hoping the attack would abate before she reached the bar. She took a handkerchief from her purse and dabbed at her forehead and mouth. The last time she'd felt like this she had spent a week in bed with a mild case of food poisoning, the result of monosodium glutamate in Chinese food.

The capsule wasn't working this time, she thought. Then put it down to the heat. By the time she met Jean, she'd be all right. She swallowed again, mouth pursing as she tasted sourness. The driver glanced in his mirror again and repeated his enquiry.

'I'm fine,' she snapped. 'Don't worry about me.'

His shrug was expressive: All right, lady. It's your funeral.

They reached 103rd and cut eastwards into the heart of the city. The traffic was worse here and a block before the cocktail bar there was a snarl-up that clogged the street ahead and the cross streets either side. The driver leant out the window to yell at a cop passing through the jammed cars. The cop yelled back something about a pile-up. A driver passed out in the heat.

'Gonna take a while, lady.'

She glanced at the Tissot and opened her purse.

'I'll walk the rest. What do I owe?'

He quoted the fare and she paid him, climbing reluctantly out of the cab. Jean hated to be kept waiting, and the snarl-up looked like it would take a lot longer to sort out than it would take her to walk the block. Even in this damnable heat.

The air was thick with exhaust fumes and the blaring of horns cut knife-like through her skull, starting up a throbbing headache that sent a dull rhythm pounding inside her head like an accompaniment to the pain in her belly. She cursed the heat and the traffic and the smell coming off the lake. She made a mental note to call the clinic and ask about the medicaments prescribed. The damn' capsules were supposed to prevent this kind of feeling, and for the money she'd paid, she expected the damn' things to work. She reached the sidewalk and made her way along in the direction of the bar. The nausea was worse now, aggravated by the motion of walking. There was a fire inside her, seeming to emanate from the pit of her stomach and climb its way through her intestines so that her bowels burned and her back ached. She paused in the temporary shelter of a storefront, letting the wash of

35

cool air from the unit mounted over the door flow over her. The coolness seemed merely to accentuate her feverishness, a sudden bout of shivering rattling her teeth as goosebumps started out on her arms. She stepped out from the storefront, her teeth clamping hard together as the sick feeling in her belly returned with greater force, and concentrated on the suddenly difficult task of walking down the street. Each step seemed to jar her, renewing the unpleasant activity inside so that she swallowed to cut off the whimper of pain threatening to burst from her lips. Her throat was dry, and when she licked her lips she tasted the saltiness of sweat and hoped her make-up wasn't running. She wondered if she had picked up one of the bugs going round and made a mental note to organize a check-up as soon as she could. The headache was worse, getting fiercer as she came closer to the source of the hold-up and the blaring of the horns got louder. There was an ambulance parked on the kerbside, a police car behind it. Both vehicles had their flashers going and the stroboscopic effect of the red and blue lights made her blink, her vision blurring.

She forced herself to walk faster, averting her eyes from the flickering glare. And the increased speed of her movement brought on a fresh attack. This time it was really bad. The pain was no longer a thing she could ignore: it had become a crescendo inside her, forcing her to groan out loud as she pushed through the crowd watching the incident on the street. A man swore at her as she bumped against him, and the sudden outburst of oral violence seemed to snap something in her mind. She began to cry. Then to curse as she realized the tears would spoil the carefully-planned effect of her make-up. She hurried through the crowd, oblivious now of the irritation of the people she pushed aside; not caring. She saw a blue neon sign, faint in the heat haze, advertising a bar, and went inside.

It was cool in there, the air-conditioning turned up so

that she began to shiver again, the cold fighting with the heat inside her. She blinked tears from her eyes, letting her vision adjust to the dimness. There was a bar counter running down one wall, tables and chairs on the floor between that and the booths. The place was almost empty and no one paid her much attention as she hurried down the length of the room towards the haven advertised by the small neon sign at the end.

She went into the Ladies Room and slumped for a moment against the door. She was glad to find the room was empty: she didn't want anyone to see her in this condition. Moving slower now, so as not to aggravate the pain in her stomach, she went over to the mirror mounted above the wash basins. The reflection of her face gave her a shock: her eyes were red, ringed by sullen shadows, the eye-liner, shadow and gloss had smeared and run. Her cheeks seemed hollowed and her lipstick was smudged where she had pursed her lips against the pain.

My God! she thought. I look dreadful.

Then she forgot about her looks as the nausea climbed up from her stomach and she knew she had to reach a booth or vomit over the floor.

She was beginning to retch as she fumbled in her purse for coins, dropping change as she found a quarter and thumbed it into the slot. The door sprang open and she stumbled inside the cubicle, slamming the door with her elbow and only just remembering to snap the lock into place. Her hands were trembling as she lifted the seat and went down on her knees. The bowl gave off an odour of parazone that sliced into her nostrils with a ferocity that rasped at her sinuses and brought a fresh flood of tears from her eyes. Blindly, all thoughts of dignity or decorum gone now, she clutched the sides of the bowl and let the vomit come.

It came in great heaving waves, scalding up from her stomach to splatter into the water, over the sides of the bowl, over her hands. Her knuckles were white with the force of her grip on the porcelain. Her throat was raw, as though the heaving and the passage of the vomit tore at the soft membranes. She moaned, tears falling with the foul-smelling outpouring of her belly. It was hard to catch her breath through the liquid clogging her throat and her head began to spin, the aching a drumbeat pounding now. She felt moisture between her legs, trickling down her thighs, but was too wrapped in the pain of the vomiting to pay it any attention.

And then the pain in her belly reached a fresh intensity. It was as though needles probed her insides. And the needles became knives, cutting and slashing. She felt her belly was opening, torn from the inside, her intestines ripping apart. She opened her mouth to scream, but instead of sound there was a fresh gout of vomit that combined with the agony in her bowels to double her over in a trembling, pain-racked ball. Her jaw struck the edge of the lavatory seat, her teeth snapping hard together so that expensive dental work was ruined and then forgotten as the awful, searing waves of pain took over. Something exploded inside her, she could not tell if it was in her stomach or her head. Only that she had never known such agony.

She wished it would end.

It was her last thought: it did.

Bella Darleigh was a regular of *Mick's Bar*. For the past six years she had worked in Bondell's Bookshop, three doors down, and each evening at precisely 6.05 she appeared at the bar. Joe – who had inherited the place from a man called Sam, but – like Sam – saw no reason to change the name – greeted her the same way each time: he put a shot glass of bourbon on the counter, flanked it with a chaser of branch water, and said, 'Hi, Bella. How's things?' And she replied the same way each time: 'Gettin' by, Mick.' After that, Joe left her alone, replenishing her glass when it got empty and giving her the tab at exactly 8.15. By then Bella had got through between six and ten bourbons, depending on the nature of her day and the mood it had caused her to be in. She was never really drunk, but nor was she ever completely sober by the time she quit the bar and walked the five blocks back to her brownstone apartment. She always used the Ladies Room before she left. Joe liked her: she spent money on a regular basis and never made any kind of fuss.

Until tonight.

Tonight, Bella was not in a good mood. Takings at the bookstore were down and if they didn't pick up soon, her chances of a rise were about as distant as her dream of retiring to Acapulco and finding a personal beachboy. In consequence, Bella had downed her ten bourbons and was feeling the effects. More to the immediate point, she was feeling the effects of the branch water chasers.

She settled her tab and rose – a trifle unsteadily – to her feet. Clutching her somewhat battered purse, she made her way down to the end of the bar and entered the Ladies Room. Then her nostrils puckered at the smell and she thought, pigs. Someone's thrown up. Goddam drunks.

She sniffed in disgust and went into the available of the two cubicles, telling herself she'd have a word with Mick (who was really Joe) when she came out.

When she came out, she saw that the other cubicle was still occupied, and wondered if the user had passed out. The smell was really bad, like the reek coming off a Seventh Street wino. She glanced at the door, her essentially good nature getting the better of her distaste, and tapped on the peeling paintwork. There was no reply. No sound at all. She tapped again, then called, 'You all right in there?' There was no answer.

Bella shrugged and stepped back.

Her foot slithered over the tiles and she t'sked, looking down. And her eyes got very wide, forming big circles that matched the round of her opening mouth as she saw the blood coming from under the door. It was dark and thick and it was mostly the blood that was giving off the sickly smell. Bella took a step back, the tendons along her jaw tautening as her mouth got wider and a scream began to form somewhere back in her throat. Her eyes were fastened on the slick, spreading pool of blood. Her feet left marks, dark red, across the tiles. She struck the edge of a wash basin and the physical contact broke the numbing shock of horror that was paralysing her vocal cords.

Her scream was loud and shrill and long.

She was shaking and pointing as Joe crashed through the door, freckled face a mixture of worry and irritation. It went pale and slack as he saw what she was pointing at.

He said, 'Oh my God! Oh, Christ!'

There was a knot of customers gathering around the entrance and professional concern worked to calm Joe's panic. He spread his arms wide, trying to block their view and shouted, 'It's OK. Everything's OK. Just calm down. A little accident, that's all. Just an accident.'

Bella's screaming had died away to a husky gasping and Joe grabbed her, dragging her away from the wash basin to steer her out into the bar. He shut the door on the curious faces and stared at the blood, wondering what the hell he should do next. Then, not much wanting to do it, but knowing he should, he went into the cubicle Bella had recently vacated and clambered onto the seat. He grabbed the top of the dividing wall and peered over.

The sight beyond the wall robbed his face of its last vestiges of colour. The woman he remembered noticing earlier was slumped over the seat, her head hanging down into the bowl. There was vomit matting her hair, and her hands, flung out to either side as though she had clawed at the porcelain and the walls, were bloodstained where her nails had broken. Her knees were drawn up close to her belly, jutting her posterior at an acute angle. The seat of her skirt was dark and thick with blood. It covered her legs and the floor, spilling out beneath the door. Flies were buzzing inside the cubicle.

Joe got down from the precarious elevation and went out to the wash basins. He ran a tap, splashing cold water over his face. He wanted to take deep breaths, but the stench inside the room persuaded him against that recourse and he contented himself with the water. Then he went out into the bar, ignoring the waiting crowd as he eased his pot belly around the angle and lifted the telephone from under the counter. Emergency numbers were pasted to the overhang of the bar and he dialled the local precinct, blurting out his report to a bored desk sergeant who promised to get a squad car and an ambulance over as fast as traffic and the heatwave permitted.

Joe set the telephone down and poured himself a generous measure of Old Crow. He swallowed it fast and then fetched the *Out of Order* sign from a drawer. Pinned it to the door of the Ladies Room. Locked the door.

The crowd was larger now, augmented by the influx of early evening drinkers. Joe surprised them by announcing a round on the house. Bella didn't surprise him by joining in.

After a while they heard sirens approaching, and then the bright amber and blue of the squad car's warning lights began to flash against the glass frontage of *Mick's Bar*. Joe took a deep breath and got ready to go back into the bloody room.

4

Mike Stoner stared at Eddison's back. The administrator was going through an English phase: Thomson twills creasing neatly over polished black Oxfords, a Shetland plaid coat in muted check, cotton oxford shirt and quiet tie. The man had his back to Stoner, staring out the wall-to-wall window that commanded a view over the interior court of the hospital. It was a pose with which Stoner was familiar. It meant that Eddison had something on his mind.

He waited for the small, balding man to face him again.

'It's a problem,' Eddison murmured. And the way he said it, Stoner knew it meant, it's your problem.

'Why?' he asked, blandly innocent. 'An autopsy's normal in these circumstances. Regs.'

'I know.' Eddison turned from the window, his pale face blank. 'But Laurence Anders could make a lot of trouble. He knows people on the board.'

'So let them explain procedures,' said Stoner.

Eddison smiled: a bad sign.

'Look,' he said; condescending. 'The less fuss, the better we can go about our business. All I'm asking is that you speak to the man.'

'I did.' Stoner shrugged, wondering what Eddison's coat had cost. 'I told him what I saw and I told him there'd be an autopsy.'

'And Anders didn't want one.' Irritation lent an edge to the administrator's voice. 'He wants no embarrassment. No fuss.'

'It's a mite late, isn't it?' Stoner kept the grin off his face. 'I saw the report this morning.'

'I know.' Eddison lifted a red coded file from his desk.

42

'She died of massive blood loss, mainly from the collapsed womb and bowel systems. Blood samples show AB. She was pregnant.'

'And we don't know why it happened,' Stoner finished for him. 'Is that what bothers you?'

'No.' Eddison shook his head. Then, absently: 'The blood was AB. Laurence Anders is O.'

Stoner was no longer able to suppress the grin. 'Is that it? The foetus didn't match her husband's blood type? He wasn't the father?'

'That's not it,' Eddison snapped, dropping the file. 'What the dead woman did, or with whom, is no business of ours. I just don't want Anders stirring things up. We've got appropriations coming up for review, and the less public hassle we get, the better.'

'I still don't see where I come in,' argued Stoner. 'All I did was check she was dead and watch her loaded.'

'You spoke to him before.' Eddison flicked a thread of lint from his cuff. 'He knows your name. You've experienced doctor fixation before.'

'Sure.' Stoner nodded. 'But what can I tell him that you haven't?'

'Reassure him,' said Eddison, smiling again now. 'Tell him his wife never knew what hit her. Tell him the autopsy was inconclusive. And that there will be no further tests.'

'Really?' Stoner's attention was caught now. 'You're not checking?'

Eddison shook his head, looking smug: a man one jump ahead.

'No. I've already signed the release.' He glanced at the Rolex on the underside of his wrist. 'The body's probably been collected already. It's to be a cremation, I understand. And a sealed coffin.'

Stoner frowned. 'That's kind of mysterious, isn't it? Why all the secrecy?'

'I don't know.' Eddison eased himself into the leather chair behind his desk. 'And I don't care. What I do care about is the hospital. If Anders gets it in his head to make trouble, it could be awkward – it doesn't matter that we did everything by the book.'

'So I'm just doing a PR job.' Stoner stared straight into the administrator's pale blue eyes. 'Keeping the customers happy.'

'If you want to put it that way,' said Eddison, confident now. 'I'd prefer to think that you're pursuing an ancillary path – consoling the bereaved.'

'All right.' Stoner sighed, knowing when he was beaten. 'I'll call him.'

'No.' Eddison shook his head. 'He wants to meet you. In person.'

Stoner nodded, a sudden random thought crossing his mind. If he spoke with Anders, he might just be able to discover something more about the dead woman. Maybe a clue to her mysterious death.

'I'll fix it up,' he said. 'Is that all?'

'Yes.' Eddison nodded. 'Thank you.'

Stoner got up and went out of the office. Fay was in the anteroom, typing. She smiled as he came out.

'You survived, then.'

'Sure.' Stoner grinned at her. 'I'm the new PR man around here. Do me a favour?'

When she nodded, he asked her to call Laurence Anders and make an appointment, waiting as she dialled the number and engaged in a brief conversation.

'He'll see you this afternoon,' she said when she had replaced the receiver. 'At 4.00. His office.'

Stoner glanced at his watch (a Jean Renet given by Fay) and said, 'Fine. Anyone wants me between 3.30 and tomorrow, tell them I'm out PR-ing.'

'Be back sooner,' Fay smiled. 'I'll be waiting.'

Stoner came around the desk and kissed her on the cheek.

'I'll see you back home.'

* * *

Anders' offices were located in the centre of town, with a view over the Trinity River. The building was sixteen storeys high, and Anders' personal office was on the fifteenth floor. Stoner wondered if this was an indication of the hierarchy of the advertising agency: the closer to the top floor, the higher you were on the salary scale. Certainly, the outer office was plush. It was panelled in oak, with leather easy chairs positioned so that anyone waiting had a choice between watching the secretary – who was well worth watching – or admiring the discreet displays of the agency's successful campaigns. Stoner didn't have long to admire either because he was ushered into the sanctum within minutes of arriving.

The inner office was even more luxurious. The carpet was the kind made you feel a machete could be useful for crossing it and the Mondrian on the wall looked no more like a print than did the Braque. The leather of the chair Anders offered him was real, discreetly lit by the adjustable spotlight positioned behind the desk in such a way that Anders remained partially in shadow. Maybe, thought Stoner cynically, this was how they persuaded clients into spending money. Eddison would have loved it.

'A drink?'

Laurence Anders was a big man; a healthy-looking thirty-plus. Thick, black hair covered his skull and his pink cheeks gave off a faint aroma of Givenchy. He wore a black suit that looked like it came from the expensive levels of Nieman Marcus and a black silk tie. His shirt was dazzlingly white, the cuffs fastened with small gold links.

Stoner said, 'Thanks. Jack Daniels on ice.'

Anders went to a massive globe and slid North America and most of Europe out of sight to expose a selection of bottles. He filled a glass with Jack Daniels and added three ice cubes from a separate freezer built into the wall behind the globe. Poured himself a straight Scotch from a bottle with Glen something curling around kilted bagpipers on the label, and sat down behind the desk.

'What exactly do you want to know?' Stoner asked.

Anders shrugged, fidgeting with his glass.

'Eddison read me the autopsy report before you arrived. How much farther will that go?'

'If you mean who'll see it,' said Stoner, 'Eddison. Me. The girl who typed it. The police department.'

'That's routine, I suppose?'

For some reason Anders sounded worried.

'Routine,' Stoner confirmed. 'We have to keep a record. So does the DPD. There's no reason anyone else should see it. Nor any reason anyone should take any interest.'

'Good.' Anders swallowed whisky. 'I suppose I'm being paranoid, but I hate the thought of strangers – how can I put it? – pawing over Marianne's death. Can you understand that?'

'I guess,' murmured Stoner. 'You can rest assured it will go no farther than routine procedures demand. I believe the body has already been released for cremation.'

Anders nodded. 'I wanted to get it over with as swiftly as possible. Best to cut loose ends.'

Stoner wondered why the man wasn't more concerned with finding out why his wife had died.

'Do you mind if I ask some questions?' he said, and wondered why the executive looked suddenly evasive.

'No.' Anders' reply was slow in coming. 'But I reserve the right not to answer them.'

'Sure.' Stoner sipped his drink. 'Your wife was pregnant.'

'A few months, yes.' Anders went over to the globe and topped his glass. 'Was that the cause of her death?'

'Possibly.' Stoner wondered how to phrase the questions he wanted to ask. 'The autopsy was inconclusive. The kind where the official CoD – cause of death – goes down as "heart stoppage due to blood loss". Was she taking any kind of drugs?'

'Nothing more than prescribed. By the finest doctors available.' Anders drank more Scotch.

'Can you give me their names?' Stoner asked.

'I'm sorry.' Anders shook his head. 'I'd prefer not to.'

'Why not?' Stoner saw his PR image go wafting out the window.

'Discretion,' said Anders. 'I'd prefer to put the affair behind me. If I can. Besides, why involve anyone else?'

'It might happen again,' said Stoner. 'I'd like to be able to prevent it if I can.'

'I doubt I can help in that,' said Anders, shifting slightly in his chair so that less of his face was visible. 'There was nothing out of the ordinary in the treatments or the medicine.'

'Treatments?' said Stoner; quickly. 'What treatments?'

'Prescribed treatments.' Anders said it a shade too quickly. 'I assure you there was nothing untoward.'

'I'm not doubting that,' said Stoner. 'But I'd like . . .'

'I'm sorry.' Anders cut him short. 'I don't feel I can answer any more questions. I appreciate your coming over, but I have to ask you to go now.'

Stoner nodded, setting his unfinished drink down on the desktop. Thinking: You appreciate my telling you no one will hear about it. Nor ask any more questions. At least, not officially. He kept his thoughts to himself as Anders came around the desk and shook hands.

'Thank you, Doctor Stoner. I really do appreciate your time. If there's anything I can do . . .'

He left the sentence hanging as he walked Stoner to the big oak panelled door and ushered him through. Stoner went out with his hands in his pockets and his mind pondering the curious attitude of the recently bereaved executive. He rode the elevator down to the first floor and stepped out of the cool comfort of the glossy building into the heat on the streets. His doctor's tag had saved him from a parking fine, and he climbed into the Mustang and pulled out into the traffic flow, heading back in the direction of his apartment.

* * *

'It doesn't make sense.' He lounged in an easy chair as Fay mixed whisky sours. 'The man just lost his wife, but he doesn't want to know why she died. That don't make sense, nohow.'

'Why not?' Fay handed him a glass. 'He could be in shock. Perhaps he just wants to forget the whole thing. Perhaps the baby wasn't his.'

'It couldn't have been.' Stoner sipped the sharply refreshing alcohol. 'The blood groups rule that out.'

'So perhaps she had an affair.' Fay shrugged, easing her legs under her as she sat down on the floor. 'Perhaps that's why.'

'Maybe.' Stoner frowned thoughtfully. 'But he said she was under medical care. Made a big point of it.'

'I read about AID a while ago,' Fay murmured. 'Perhaps they were having a test tube baby. That could embarrass him – admitting he was sterile.'

'Yeah.' Stoner nodded. 'Perhaps. But I still got a funny feeling.'

'Mike.' There was a hint of warning in her voice. 'It's not your business. Don't make waves.'

Stoner looked at her sharply, sensing something behind her words. Something he knew she would prefer not to say out loud. When he spoke again, his voice had an edge to it.

'Are you warning me off, Fay?'

She shrugged, blonde hair bobbing around her oval face. In the light filtering through the drapes her eyes were tinged with grey, the shift in colouration reminding him of clouds gathering over the ocean.

'I wasn't going to say anything, but Eddison was dropping hints. They were pretty broad.'

'So go on, tell me.' The slight irritation he had felt left him as he recognized the concern in her voice, in her eyes. 'Maybe I can take a hint.'

'There wasn't anything specific,' she said, looking down at her glass, then up at his face again. 'But he made it pretty clear that he didn't want any of this to go any farther.'

'He near as dammit told me that,' grunted Stoner. 'Influential husband and hospital publicity. All that stuff.'

'More than that,' Fay murmured; reluctant. 'He's worried about what Anders might do to our reputation, sure. But he let me know that if it went any farther the blame would land on you. It was a kind of warning: hands off, I guess.'

'The bastard!' Stoner's brown eyes flashed. 'What the hell does he think he's playing at?'

'He'd call it protecting the hospital,' said Fay. 'The hospital's standing against the career of one doctor.'

'And I'd lose,' Stone muttered. 'If I make waves.'

'I think he'd drown you,' Fay nodded. 'He could, you know.'

Stoner nodded, face clouding as he thought about it. Whatever the cause of Marianne Anders' death, there was now an effective seal set on any further investigation. The autopsy report had been precise and brief. It had accorded with the legal requirements appertaining in the event of death under unusual circumstances. It had stated the cause of the woman's demise – haemorrhage – and nothing more. There had been no further investigation, nothing more than was legally required, and no real explanation of the cause of the blood loss. Now, with the corpse released for cremation, there was no chance of deeper probing. And for some reason politics had entered the scene: Eddison was making it very clear that Laurence Anders called the shots. And the widower had made it equally clear that he wanted no further questions asked.

Stoner wondered if he was getting paranoid. Perhaps Fay was right. Perhaps it was just that the man wanted his wife disposed of with as much dignity as was left her, with as little fuss as possible. For purely personal reasons.

'I know he could,' he admitted.

'So you'll go along?' Fay said it a trifle too quickly, and

Stoner knew that she was thinking again about that great career she had planned for him.

'I guess,' he said. 'There's not much else I can do, is there?'

'Not really,' Fay smiled.

Stoner climbed to his feet, suddenly restless. In a way, he wished there had been some other doctor on hand to take that goddam emergency call. A good, solid, reliable doctor who wouldn't have even dreamed of making waves. Who would have checked the body for signs of life and been content to put his name on the death certificate without thinking further about it. Just consigned Marianne Anders to the limbo of the records department and gone on about his business. But there hadn't been. It had been him who saw the corpse. And he could still recall the smell. Remember the way her face had looked. It was just like a troublesome tooth: not serious enough to warrant immediate concern, but niggling enough it was hard to resist probing. Just to see what happened.

He emptied his glass and said, 'Let's go out.'

Fay nodded. There was an obstinate core to the man she loved, and half the time it was something she admired. The other half, it was something that worried her. Mike could have such a great career if only he could accept the rules of the game. And succeeding in medicine – as in any other line of business – meant playing by the rules. Break them, and you could be destroyed. It was the same obstinacy that made him refuse her father's offer of help – a key to the heights of success. His own practice. His own clinic, even. If only he could unbend that little bit. It was something she worked on with a patience that came close to matching Stoner's own obstinacy. Now she could see that obstinacy pushing him into a confrontation with Eddison that only the administrator could win. If Eddison chose, he could destroy Mike's career with a few well-placed words, an unfavourable report. Somehow she had to steer Mike away from that, and right now going out seemed the best way.

'Where?' she asked brightly. 'Do I dress?'

'Let's go find Rafe,' he said. 'I want to talk to him.'

Fay stifled her sigh, knowing that an objection would only prompt her lover to go ahead. Perhaps Rafe would talk him down.

'Fine.' She smiled, moving towards the bedroom.

Antrim was slouched in a booth in his favourite bar. His close-cropped hair was ruffled and his tie was tugged down from his open shirt collar. His craggily good-looking face was morose, lighting only slightly as he saw Stoner and Fay approaching.

'What you drinkin'?' he greeted them, his voice blurred a little.

Stoner asked for a beer, and Fay said she would have the same. Antrim called for a pitcher and another Jack Daniels. A double.

'What's the trouble?' Stoner recognized the signs of dissatisfaction in his friend. 'Another argument?'

Antrim shrugged his broad shoulders. He had been a good quarter back in his college days, and still retained the solidly-muscled frame of a football player, despite years of heavy drinking. Since his divorce he had seemed bent on killing himself with liquor, that and his job on the *Dallas Tribune* being his only interests.

'Yeah.' He nodded, then chuckled cynically. 'I got a lead on those dead sheep. You remember? Three hundred found dead over in Nevada? Big hassle for about nine days, then it's all quiet on the goddam western front.'

Stoner nodded and poured beer.

'I did some checking,' Antrim continued. 'It was fuckin' obvious from the start. They were herding the woolly bastards right on the edge of the old Army testing zone. Only there haven't been any tests recently enough to kill the things. I checked with a guy I know out that way, and he came up with some interesting facts. Like there's a stream supposed to have been sealed off that runs out of the zone through the area they found the sheep. It's sealed off well enough now, but last winter there was a big storm. Flash floods all over. Shepherd said he saw water in the stream bed. It's dry now, but put two and two together and what do you get?'

He emptied his glass and called for another before answering his own question.

'You get a botched job on the sealing, that's what. You get fucking poison water seeping out and killing three hundred head of mobile lamb chops.'

'So you get a story,' Stoner said. 'What's the problem?'

Antrim chuckled again. 'Michael, my dear, innocent boy, you do not get a story. Not if the government's dropped enough compensation on the shepherds it's choked them. Not if you've got some goddam faceless pissant bureaucrat calling your editor to suggest it might not be in the public's interest to start a panic. Not if your editor's had his balls cut off. Then you do not have a story.'

He lifted his glass, staring moodily at the amber liquid.

'And if you wish to continue buying this lovely stuff in sufficient quantities to blur the hard edges of unpleasant reality, you accept all that. You keep your mouth shut and your typewriter silent. You go out and get drunk.'

'Maybe it's for the best,' said Fay. 'After all, the government should know what it's doing.'

'Ah!' Antrim turned towards her, face creasing in a sarcastically benign smile that almost camouflaged the bitterness of his reply. 'There speaks the voice of respectable America. Let us not ask questions. Let us accept whatever shit the government throws at us.'

'Easy, Rafe,' Stoner warned. 'Fay's got a mind of her own.'

'I know.' Antrim's smile became apologetic. 'I'm sorry, Fay. I'm not getting at you – you're just the nearest easy target. But you see what I mean? The point is, I don't believe the government *does* know what it's fucking about with. I believe it's divided up into so many self-contained departments it's lost sight of its duties. I believe that people have the right to know, whether the news is good or bad. At least Joe Public should get a chance to decide for himself. Deny him that right, and you've got a system that's not much different from all those things the same government says we have to stop in other countries. I say: let's clean up our own house before we go shovelling shit overseas.'

He sat back, smiling genuinely now. Emptying his glass. Behind him a man in cowboy boots and a beat-up stetson pressed buttons on the jukebox. George Jones started to extol the joys of trucking.

'So you got told to forget it, and you came out to get boozed.' Fay leant forwards across the table. 'Is that responsible?'

'No,' said Antrim. 'But it's consolation. It was made very clear to me that if I failed to keep my flapping mouth closed tight I should very soon be pounding that time-worn path between the newspaper offices. With very little chance of anyone welcoming me in.'

'Join the club,' murmured Stoner. 'I got the same treatment.'

'What?' Antrim's face was suddenly interested. 'Dissent in the hallowed halls of medicine?'

Stoner laughed, and told him about Marianne Anders. About Eddison, and the dead woman's husband.

'You see?' The newspaperman's voice was triumphant. 'There are big hush-ups and there are little hush-ups. An ascending power scale that effectively blocks off honest investigation. I didn't think medicine worked that way.'

'Dammit!' Fay spoke before Stoner got a chance. 'A woman died. That's sad, but it happens every day in Dallas. Her husband wants her quietly buried – sorry, cremated – for personal reasons, and it gets built up into something it's not.'

53

'Maybe,' said Stoner. 'Or maybe not. I don't like it.'

'Nor do I,' said Antrim. 'Let's have another drink and console one another.'

Fay pursed her lips as he shouted for more beer and a fresh Jack Daniels. Merle Haggard began to sing about his love affair with trains, and she resigned herself to an evening's steady drinking as Stoner and Antrim launched into a discussion about the morality of government influence on news media. At least, she told herself, it gave Mike a chance to get things off his chest. Maybe he could talk it out and forget about it. Rafe seemed to be succeeding.

They stayed in the bar until close on ten, then Antrim suggested they find somewhere to eat. It took another half hour to make up their minds, and then they piled into Stoner's Mustang and headed for a Chinese place on McKinnon Street.

Antrim drank beer with his food, but Stoner and Fay took tea. By the time they were finished it was close on midnight and the newspaperman was distinctly unsteady on his feet. They got him into the car and Stoner drove him to the furnished apartment he rented in the outskirts. They waited until he got the door open – not without difficulty – and then headed for Stoner's place. It was a warm night, the heatwave gripping the east and south of the country prolonging the heat of the day so that they drove with the windows down, enjoying the rush of air over their faces. Stoner detoured via White Rock Lake, parking to watch the moon reflecting off the surface of the still water.

'He'll kill himself if he goes on like this,' Fay murmured. 'Why doesn't he stop?'

Stoner shrugged, adjusting his arm about her shoulders, enjoying the scent of her hair.

'What else has he got?' he queried. 'Joan left him because she couldn't take the hours he works. Rafe's work is important to him, but it's not enough. He drinks to make up the loss.'

'Harsh words for a doctor.' Fay eased closer against him. 'You sound almost as though you approve.'

'He knows what he's doing.' Stoner stared at the rippling surface of the lake. 'I've told him what the physical consequences are, so it's his choice.'

'Leave well alone?' Fay teased him. 'He's an alcoholic, Mike.'

'You know that, I know that.' Stoner nuzzled her neck, wondering why they were discussing Rafe right now. 'But Rafe doesn't. He's just a heavy drinker. It's a classic case. It's not a question of "leave well alone". The only person who can help an alcoholic is himself. I can tell Rafe what he's doing to his body, but I can't make him want to stop.'

Like us, Fay thought. I think I know what's best for you, but I can't make you listen to my advice. All I can do is to give it and hope.

She wriggled on the seat, shifting round to fold closer into his arms, thinking, At least I can make you forget for a while.

'I got a blanket in the back,' Stoner whispered. 'Want to try it?'

Fay giggled. 'Um. That sounds like a nice idea.'

They got out of the car and spread the blanket on the still-warm grass. And forgot.

5

The letter Stoner received the next day brought it all back
in a rush. He was alone in his apartment – Fay had
arranged dinner with a girlfriend, and was planning to
return to her own place after, while Stoner anticipated
sinking a few Millers while he watched a re-run of *The
Searchers*. The letter was waiting for him in his mailbox.

He recognized the slanting hand on the envelope before
he saw the Phoenix postmark, and wondered what news
his mother had.

The bulk of it was routine. She was well, but his father
had put on a little weight since his retirement. The patch
of land they had bought was doing well, but the roof of
their house needed fixing. Neighbours sent greetings, and
they all wondered when he was coming by for a visit. The
part that caught Stoner's interest concerned someone he
hadn't thought of in years.

Her name was Betty Ramsden now – or it was the day
she died – but when Stoner had known her, she had been
Betty Willard. They had been sweethearts. Stoner had
known her since they were both in eighth grade, and in
college she had solemnly agreed to be his girl. It had been
one of those fierce, brief teenage romances that outdo in
sheer fervour the brevity of the affair, and consequently
burn themselves on the memory. They had been in love,
and for that reason and the unspoken understanding that
one day they were going to get married, Betty had – in the
parlance of the times – let him go all the way. It had been
one night in November, a chill just starting to creep into
the air so that the windows of Stoner's secondhand Dodge
were misted over as they parked out on Buena Vista and
Betty slowly removed her clothing. They had climbed into

the back of the car and spent three hours Stoner could still recall with vivid clarity. They had discovered sex together, and for that reason Betty occupied a special, indelible place in Stoner's memory.

The romance had lasted almost exactly eighteen months. Effectively up to the time Stoner left Phoenix to take up his medical studies. They had promised never to forget one another, and for the first few months they corresponded with a tender frequency. Then the letters had slowed down, and while Stoner was wondering how to tell Betty it was crazy to pretend their affair could last (a decision largely prompted by a blonde student with the longest legs Stoner had ever seen) Betty informed him that she had met someone else. Stoner knew Will Ramsden from grade school. They were not quite friends, but Ramsden's was a face seen around the Phoenix parties, someone Stoner could spend a pleasant hour or two with, without seeking out his company. He had got to know the man better since his marriage to Betty, visiting with them and discovering Will to be a thoughtful, intelligent, if somewhat conservative man. He was also extremely wealthy.

His mother's news brought all the old memories back in a rush, mingling them with Stoner's present concerns so that he came upright in his chair, his beer forgotten as he stared at the words.

'You recall young Betty?' his mother wrote. 'Will Ramsden's wife, as was? Well, Mike, she died. It was the most awful thing, and no one seems to know quite how it happened. She hadn't been too well, because Will took her off for a vacation about a year ago and then they were off again a few months after. Will told us Betty was a mite run down, mainly on account of worrying about them not having any kids.

'Well, she seemed a whole lot better after their last trip. They went up north someplace. Mountain air, Will said. And when they got back Betty just seemed to be blooming. I remember telling her one time she looked as happy

57

and healthy as a woman getting ready to give birth, and she just blushed and said it was the way Will looked after her.

'Well, Mike, they found her out near the Gila. You remember how she did that voluntary work on the Reservation? She was out there that day. Real hot, I recall. She didn't get home and Will called the PDP and the State Troopers, and Gabe Ranchette took his bike out to the Reservation and he found her car in a ditch. Betty was dead. Just like that, Mike. Gabe said she was at the wheel and there was a lot of blood, but I could tell that wasn't all the story. Gabe didn't say too much about it and I didn't like to ask Will, but I don't think anyone knows quite how she died. There wasn't a smash, and Gabe said it wasn't crazy hippies or anything like that. She'd just bled to death, it seems.'

The rest of the letter was mostly about Will and how he was coping. Stoner read it fast, not really paying much attention, his eyes drawn back to the three crucial paragraphs and those oddly significant words: *there was a lot of blood, but I could tell that wasn't all the story . . . She'd just bled to death, it seems.'*

The funeral had followed soon after. It had been a quiet, strictly family affair and there had been no further news.

Stoner held the sheets of bluish paper in his hand, eyes fixed unseeing on the television screen as the opening credits of Ford's classic Western began to unroll. John Wayne appeared on the screen and Stoner stood up as the big man spoke his first lines. He went over to the set and depressed the on/off control, still staring blankly as the picture faded and died. Then he lifted the can to his mouth and drained the last of the Millers. Went over to the refrigerator and fetched a fresh can from the six-pack. He pulled the ring and dropped it on the surface of the breakfast bar, taking the can with him as he went over to the telephone and dialled Rafe Antrim's number.

There was no answer, so he called the *Tribune*. The nightboard operator connected him with Rafe.

'Mike?' Antrim's voice was clear, not blurred with drink. 'What you doin' disturbing a working man?'

'Information.' Stoner's mind was made up now. 'I thought maybe you could get it, Rafe.'

'What kind?' Antrim asked calmly.

Stoner paused for a moment, wondering just how to phrase it. He wanted – needed – to use the information facilities available to Rafe, but he was not yet sure how much to tell the newspaperman. He wondered if he really was getting paranoid – and he didn't want to make a fool of himself.

'About dead women,' he said. 'I thought maybe you'd have something on file.'

'Hey!' Antrim laughed. 'You turning kinky, Mike? Is it necrophilia now?'

Stoner forced a chuckle he didn't feel. 'No, Rafe. I'm not sure what I'm getting at, but you remember the other night? I told you about Marianne Anders?'

A good newspaperman, Antrim said 'Yes' immediately. Stoner could hear the interest in his voice.

'I just got a letter from home,' he said slowly. 'Mom wrote me an old friend died in what sound like the same circumstances. Car off the road. Woman inside in a lot of blood. No word on why or how.'

'Where?' Antrim asked. 'What was her name?'

As Stoner gave him the information he could hear the faint scratching of Antrim's pencil. Then the newspaperman said, 'All right, I got that. What you want me to do?'

'See if you can find out whether there've been any similar reports,' Stoner said. 'Anywhere. Can you do that?'

'I guess.' Antrim grunted an affirmative. 'But it's a pretty broad spec. Any woman dead from blood loss? Even if I cut out rapes, muggings, auto accidents; all that stuff. Just keep it to unexplained causes. That's still pretty wide. Can you give me anything else? Some sort of link to narrow the field down?'

'Betty was pretty wealthy.' Stoner ransacked his mind for similarities between Betty Ramsden and Marianne Anders. 'Yeah, that could be one. The Anders woman was, what? 32? And Betty must have been around the same age. How's that?'

'Better.' Antrim was writing again. 'OK, buddy. Rich ladies around the 30 mark dead from unexplained blood loss. I'll see what I can do.'

'How long?' Stoner asked.

'Locally, a day or so,' Antrim replied. 'All over, that could take a week or two. Let me call you back.'

'Yeah, thanks. And Rafe? I think I'm going out to Phoenix. Hold onto it until I'm back, OK?'

'Whatever you say,' Antrim agreed. 'There a story in this?'

'Might be.' Stoner found himself suddenly cautious. Fay's warning about Eddison's tangentially-delivered threats came into his mind. 'I'm not sure yet. Hell! I'm not even sure what I'm doing. But I don't want to talk about it until I've got some facts.'

'The pragmatic medical mind,' chuckled Antrim. 'All right, Mike. I won't ask questions and I won't mention this to anyone. OK?'

'Yeah, thanks. I'll see you round, Rafe.'

He set the telephone down and went back to the chair. He sipped his beer thinking that he had some leave due and now was as good a time as any to take it. He'd need to clear it with Eddison, but that shouldn't be difficult; and he could get a flight to Phoenix maybe tomorrow.

After a while he got up and turned the tv on again. Wayne was talking to Scar. Playing it cagey. Stoner watched to the end of the movie then put a tape on the VCR and watched *Rio Bravo* for the eighth or ninth time. He was too keyed up to sleep.

* * *

'Mike!' Fay's tone was pitched between anger, disappointment and curiosity. 'We were going to use that time to go up to Colorado. You know Daddy said we could use the lodge.'

'I'm sorry, honey.' Stoner went on folding shirts into a small hold-all. 'But I really have to go. Old family friend. You know.'

'I know I was looking forward to Colorado,' said Fay with deliberate sulkiness. 'How long will you be?'

'A week,' Stoner said. 'No more. I promise.'

'I'll hold you to that.' Fay's pout gave way to a resigned smile. 'Move over. Those shirts will look a mess.'

Stoner moved aside and watched as she repacked his bag. For no reason he could clearly define – except, perhaps, that he was afraid she would not approve – he hadn't told Fay the reason for his visit. At least, not the real reason. He had told her a childhood friend had died suddenly and he felt he should go home as the husband was a friend. He let her think his mother had asked him to do that much. He had a midnight flight into Sky Harbor and an Avis automobile waiting for him there. Eddison had agreed to his taking leave with an alacrity that suggested he was rather pleased to see Stoner out of the way for a while. Or maybe that was just Stoner's imagination: maybe he was seeing plots behind plain, down-to-earth dislike.

He grinned as Fay zipped the hold-all and punched it irritably.

'It's not long,' he murmured, kissing her.

'Long enough,' she whispered. 'Hurry back.'

'Soon as I can.' Stoner picked up the bag. 'Want to drive me?'

Fay nodded and they went down to the car. She was an excellent driver and they reached the Dallas-Fort Worth Airport with time to spare. They waited in the airport bar until Stoner's flight was called, and then he boarded the small Boeing as Fay watched him from the observation gallery.

Soon after dawn, Stoner was behind the wheel of his rented Chevy, following the Maricopa Freeway towards the turn-off that led to the dirt road linking his parents' place.

It was a bungalow rather than the ranch his father liked to describe, but it was close enough to the old man's dream that he was happy there. The dirt road ran past three other, equally-isolated homes, and then Stoner picked up the fence surrounding the property. A windbreak of imported cedar screened the flat structure of the house, the solar panels glinting bright in the new-risen sun. A scatter of chickens ran from the vehicle's approach as Stoner went up the long tarmac drive, and an old man in a denim shirt and time-dilapidated Fryes shaded his eyes to study the visitor.

'Mike! It's good to see you, boy.'

Elmer Stoner looked older than Mike remembered. His silver hair was thinner and there was a noticeable bulge around the waistline of his levis. But his eyes were still keen behind the horn-rim spectacles and his grip as he shook his son's hand was still firm. Stoner grinned at him.

'Dad? It's good to be home.'

'Your momma's just fixin' some breakfast.' Elmer's dentures showed in a broad smile. 'She's gonna get some kinda surprise seein' you walk in.'

He grabbed Mike's bag and led the way to the kitchen.

'Dar? See who's come visitin'.'

Darlene Stoner let go the skillet she was holding over her Belling and peered shortsightedly at the doorway. Stoner thought she looked much the same. A little shorter, maybe, the way old people get smaller. A few more lines on her face, but mostly due to smiling. Her hair was still retaining some brunette colouring, and whoever fixed it for her had worked the last vestiges of that colouring in with the grey so that she looked a deal less than her near-seventy years. She whooped as she recognized her son and came across the sunlit kitchen to embrace him.

There were dust motes dancing in the shafts of sunlight

coming through the windows and the room was delicious with the smell of frying bacon and sizzling eggs. For a moment Stoner felt about nine years old again, but then he felt the frailty of his mother's body and was his full age.

'Sit down, sit down.' Darlene pulled a chair out. 'How long you stayin'?'

Stoner sat, luxuriating in the welcome, in the easy way they slipped into a natural relationship. They swapped news, chewing over new times and old. Guy Decker – remember him, Mike? Used to deliver oil? – was retired; gone to California to live with his daughter and her husband. And old Willy Dunbar down at the Lodge Pole? Sold up and moved to a retirement village out near Flagpole. Young Frank Comsett had opened a market and was doing nicely, thank you. And the milch cow was doing well. And nothing much had changed.

Except Betty Ramsden was dead.

Stoner worked the conversation around to that. And his father frowned and said, 'Funny, that. Gabe was kinda pale around the gills when he told me, but he still didn't talk much. And you know how Gabe loves to jaw.'

'Shock,' said Darlene firmly. 'Must have given him some kinda shock.'

Stoner wondered what it took to shock a State Trooper with ten years service.

'Will took it hard, of course,' Elmer continued. 'He worshipped that girl. Kinda fortunate, I guess, they didn't have no kids.'

'Who performed the autopsy?' Stoner asked. 'Doc Carter?'

'I guess.' His father shrugged. 'Wasn't much more said about it. Piece in the local, of course. But after that, she was just buried and we all figgered it was best to leave it be. Will don't speak of it none, and that's his right.'

Stoner nodded, and let the talk drift away to other subjects. He assured them that Fay was well. Would be visiting again when they both had time. And yes, he was

63

doing all right at the hospital. Was staying there until he decided exactly what he wanted to do. No, he hadn't accepted the Nicholas' offer – his parents let that one drop, knowing his independent streak.

They talked through breakfast, then Stoner took a shower and dumped his things in the room they kept for him. He changed into levis and a workshirt and spent the rest of the day helping his father around the place. That night he took them to the Palomino, out on Stephen Mather, where they ate steak and listened to mediocre country bands.

The next day he drove over to the Ramsden place.

Will Ramsden was a whipcord-thin man, his prematurely grey hair lending him a solemnity that belied his easy sense of humour. Little of that showed, however, as he shook hands with Stoner and accepted his condolences.

'I guess you felt pretty close to her,' he murmured as he ushered Mike to a chair and poured two healthy jiggers of tequila. 'You bein' sweethearts an' all.'

'Yeah.' Stoner nodded as he accepted the drink. 'It was a shock.'

Ramsden's face looked old as his hair and he took a long swallow before speaking again.

'The goddamdest shock I ever got. She was doin' fine until it happened.'

'Ma said she'd been ill,' Stoner ventured. 'Said you'd been on some kind of health vacation.'

'Yeah. That's right.'

Had Ramsden said it a little too quickly? Or was that Stoner's imagination?

'What was it?' he asked quietly: old friend and doctor.

'I don't know.' Ramsden's hands tightened around his glass, and for a moment Stoner thought it might break under the pressure of his grip. 'All I know is she was alive, an' now she's dead. That's all I need to know, Mike. She's dead.'

His face clamped shut, the set of his lips and the

narrowing of his eyes warning Stoner against saying anything more. The reaction reminded the doctor of Laurence Anders' attitude: there was the same refusal to discuss the bereavement in anything more than the most general terms. The same off-limits feeling. Stoner made some more appropriate noises, meaning them, and then left Will.

Two days later he succeeded in buttonholing Doc Carter.

There was a bond between the two men, not diminished by the years separating them or the long intervals between their conversations. David Carter had sparked Stoner's interest in medicine, encouraging it as the boy showed aptitude. Even schooling him a little whenever his busy rural surgery allowed. Now he was an old man, but still making his rounds of the outlying homesteads. Because, he said, all the youngsters are interested in is making money in the cities. No offence intended, of course, but you try getting a doctor to drive out one night in a rainstorm. Medicine's gotten to be money, but that ain't where the dog squats. Medicine's people. And people need tending, rich or poor. No matter where they live.

Stoner felt he knew the old man well enough to ask him outright.

'What killed Betty Ramsden?' he asked as Carter sipped his third Lone Star and the jukebox began to play Guy Clark's *South Coast of Texas*. 'No one seems to know.'

Carter's tanned face crinkled into a myriad weatherbeaten lines. 'Me included,' he said. 'She'd had some kind of haemorrhage. The autopsy didn't show much. No more'n you'd expect in a pregnant woman.'

'Pregnant?' Stoner's eyes fixed on the old man's face. 'I thought they were childless.'

'Hell!' Carter shook his head. 'I guess I shouldn't've told you that. But what the hell? You're a doctor, I'm a doctor. So: Yeah, Betty was about three months gone.'

'Will didn't tell me,' Stoner murmured.

'He wouldn't,' said Carter. 'Thing like that, it's kinda personal.'

'Can you tell me?' Stoner decided to lay his cards on the table. 'There was a woman over in Dallas died much the same way. She was around Betty's age and she was pregnant. Died from blood loss.'

Carter's green eyes narrowed down. He took a long pull on his beer, then stared hard at Stoner's face as though making up his mind about something.

'This official?' he asked.

'No,' said Stoner. 'Why?'

Carter shrugged. 'I don't know. I couldn't figger out why Betty haemorrhaged. Wanted some more tests, but Will put the clamps on. Not like Will, that. But he used his money to get things done real quick. No more'n the standard autopsy report and no questions asked beyond that. Got her buried fast as decency allowed. I thought maybe you was doing some kind of investigation.'

'Personal only,' murmured Stoner. 'I don't like puzzles any more than you. When I heard about Betty, I thought I'd come ask a few questions.'

'But you can't get too many answers?' Carter grinned. 'Mightn't be anything, Mike. Just a grieving man wanted to put it behind him fast as he can.'

'Maybe,' Stoner admitted. 'Fay said the same thing. But you weren't happy, Dave.'

'No.' Carter shook his head. 'I'm like you. Or I taught you to be like me, I don't know which. But I don't like medical mysteries. I figger if I can solve one, then I might just stand a better chance of helping the next one.'

'So explain,' Stoner urged. 'Tell me why Will never mentioned she was pregnant. Nor anyone else.'

'No one else knew.' Carter paused as the barkeep brought them two more Lone Stars. 'Will was sterile, you see. They was both worried about it. Will felt his manhood was threatened – maybe that's why he said nothing –

66

and Betty was getting depressed. I told them to adopt, if it was kids they wanted, but Betty wanted her own. So I made them a suggestion.'

He paused, sucking on his beer, then spoke again in a lowered voice. Stoner leant closer to catch the words.

'I told them if they wanted natural kids and Will couldn't father them, then they should think about artificial insemination. They didn't take too much to the idea, not at first. But they were both intelligent people for all Will comes on like a downhome redneck at times. They come back and said they'd like to check it out. I gave them a list of the places I knew about and they arranged it. Settled on a place called the Walters Institute, somewhere in Oregon. It was a mite out of my field, so I didn't have much to do with it beyond putting up the idea. They got the name of the place from some people they knew, and after it was done I just gave Betty the standard check-ups.'

'You think that was it?' Stoner forgot his beer. 'Some kind of miscarriage?'

'Way she looked it was more like a botched abortion.' Carter's mouth turned down at the edges. 'Like one of the old squaws out at the Reservation had been at her.'

Stoner got a sudden, unpleasantly vivid image of Marianne Anders sitting rigid in the Porsche.

'Yeah?' he prompted.

'Not much more to tell,' said Carter. 'She'd bled to death. Must've hit her real sudden. I guess the pain made her go off the road. God knows how long she was there all alone. Just bleeding and dying. There were placental fluids in the blood. Some trace of sedative, but nothing out of the ordinary. She was about three months gone, so there wasn't enough of the foetus left to show any irregularities. That's about all.'

He paused again, shaking his head at the memory, his face twisting in distaste as though he took personal affront at the injustice of the death.

'It was the damn' smell got me,' he murmured. 'You

know that smell you get when you're delivering a baby? It was like that. Seemed so damn' wrong, somehow. That's a smell I always associate with life, but it was there when Betty died.'

The image of Marianne Anders returned to Stoner's mind. The smell was in his nostrils again. But this time there was a linked memory with it. He drank beer, trying to pinpoint what it had been Carter had said that was tugging at his memory cells.

Betty was pregnant. Seeded in some clinic that sounded like it specialized in AID. And – hell! Yes! That was it! The memory was out in front now.

'The clinic,' he said. 'The clinic she went to. What was it called?'

'The Walters Institute.' Carter looked curious. 'Why?'

The Walters Institute.

Tasteful lettering. Dark brown on very pure white paper.

A card.

Just one more card.

In Marianne Anders' purse.

'They went to the same place.' He said it slowly: a man on the verge of an idea. Not formed yet, but the pieces making a pattern of some kind. Not large, not clear. But there, beginning to come out of the random data. 'Betty went to the Walters Institute and so did Marianne Anders.'

'That's not so unusual,' said Carter. 'If the Anders woman was wealthy, why shouldn't she have gone to the same place? Will wouldn't've had Betty go anywhere but the best. Maybe the other feller thought the same way.'

Stoner nodded. It was logical: the wealthy tended to congregate in the same areas because their money pushed them in those directions. It could be nothing more than coincidence. Will Ramsden and Laurence Anders had both sought the best for their childless wives, so maybe the Walters Institute was the best. It could be nothing, or it could be another little piece of whatever jigsaw he was playing with.

What had Rafe said? *Some sort of link to narrow the field down.*

So OK, here was another link. Betty Ramsden and Marianne Anders were both well off. They were both around thirty. They were both pregnant. And if the card in Marianne Anders' purse meant anything, they had both attended the Walters Institute.

'Excuse me a while, Dave.' He slid off the bar stool. 'I want to make a call.'

He went over to the 'phone booth and asked for a person-to-person to be put through to Rafe Antrim – he checked his watch – yeah, at the *Dallas Tribune.*

'I don't have anything yet,' Antrim said when they were connected.

'I do, though,' Stoner told him. 'There's another link. A place called the Walters Institute. I think it may be up north. I think both women may have been there.'

'The Walters Institute. Hold on.' Stoner waited as Antrim wrote it down. 'What's that?'

'I think it's some kind of exclusive clinic,' said Stoner. 'It handles artificial insemination.'

'Test tube babies?' Antrim's voice showed interest. 'That's not new, Mike. Unless something's going wrong.'

'I don't know.' Stoner fed more coins into the box as the operator warned him his time was running out. 'Maybe; maybe not. It might just be coincidence.'

'Of such fabric are stories made,' said Antrim. 'I'll see what I can find out. But Mike? I want to know what this is all about.'

'Sure,' said Stoner. 'When I get back. See what you can dig up for me, will you?'

'You got it,' Antrim sounded thoughtful now. 'I have that old familiar feeling, buddy. I want a story out of this.'

'When I get back,' Stoner repeated. And put the receiver down.

Carter's face was curious as he returned to the bar.

'I asked a friend to check,' Stoner told him. 'To find out what he can about the Walters Institute.'

Carter chuckled. 'What's to find out, Mike? It'll be some very expensive and highly reputable commercial outfit. What's that going to tell you?'

'I don't know,' Stoner said. 'I really don't know.'

6

The woman sat admiring the reflection of sunlight off the silver coffee service. The light streamed through the picture window, transforming the silk drapes to the colour of fresh cream. Beyond the window the grounds of the house ran down to Dawson Creek, where a stand of carefully planted timber shut off the view of the outskirts of Bâton Rouge. A horse snickered over towards the creek, and the woman smiled as she recognized the Arab mare her husband would describe as an investment, she as his hobby. It didn't matter who was right – they had money enough that Frank could indulge his whims. And if pretending to be a horse breeder relaxed him, then it was a fair exchange.

She looked back at the table as a negro maid entered the room, awaiting permission to remove the breakfast things, and nodded. The maid began to clear away and the woman rose to her feet, the soft folds of her peignoir swirling about her. She was a tall, healthy-looking woman, whose age was difficult to ascertain. Regular exercise – the horses were very good in that department – and equally regular visits to beauticians kept her looking and feeling fit. She was attractive without being pretty, making the most of what nature had given her and helping it along where necessary. Frank liked to say – when she was feeling low – that pretty fades, attractive gets better. She reassured herself in the bedroom, slipping out of the peignoir and the complementing nightgown to stand naked before the big mirror. Like the breakfast room, the bedroom was lit by the morning sunshine, and the image in the mirror met with her approval. Her hair was cut fashionably short, an almost boyish cut, with highlights

71

accentuating the rich auburn. Her nose was a fraction too long, but large eyes and a generous mouth made up for that slight deficiency. Sufficiently that she had decided against plastic surgery. Her neck was slender; unlined. The musculature of her body was that of an athlete: sufficient muscle tone to keep her trim without developing into truly noticeable cording. She studied her breasts. They were not enlarged yet, but her nipples seemed a little bigger. That was probably her imagination, she decided, and if not, what the hell? She had good tits. Waist and hips were fine, too. Slim and smooth, the skin still showing the tan she had picked up in the Bahamas. Her legs were her best point: long and shapely, firm about the thighs and nicely rounded on the calves. She turned her back to the mirror, looking over her shoulder to study her buttocks. They, too, were in good condition: firm, showing no sign of slackening.

She smiled, thinking that at 29 she was maybe worrying about her body a little early. But, as her mother had always told her, looks were a girl's first asset. Intelligence, money, anything else came second. And it was doubly important she keep herself in trim now. Not just for Frank's sake, but now for the baby's. The doctors had told her she had nothing to worry about. Just keep up the exercises they prescribed and keep on taking the pills; everything was going to be all right.

She hoped it was. She had been married seven years now and looking after Frank's two children by his first marriage, and that only when they came home during the vacations, was not enough. She had always wanted children, and it had come as a shock to them both when Frank was told he was no longer capable. The fall from the stallion her father had presented as part of the wedding present had done something to his insides that had rendered him incapable of fathering any more offspring. It had taken one bad year for Frank to come to terms with that, and two more before they got around to agreeing that maybe artificial insemination was the answer. As her pyschoanalyst had pointed out, if they could both accept the irrelevant fact that the child growing in her womb didn't happen to be Frank's, but might just as well be, then it should bring them closer together. And would – in the psychoanalyst's opinion – be very good for her as a female. So they had made the decision and set about some discreet enquiries. The result had been a trip to Oregon and a series of tests that left her wondering if it was such a good idea after all. Then she – or, rather, *they* – had been accepted and she had felt as excited as the day she entered Bryn Mawr as a preppy. Since then they hadn't looked back, and now she was three and a half months pregnant.

And still looking good.

There were no obvious signs. From time to time she got a craving for shrimp creole or T-bone with excesses of maitre d' butter, but that was no bad thing so long as she kept it in check. She had experienced a few bouts of nausea, usually first thing in the morning, once during a dinner party, but the pills they had given her seemed to take care of that, quelling the unpleasant feelings in her stomach as effectively as promised. All in all, things couldn't be better.

She glanced at the crucifix on the wall above the bed, thinking that she should give thanks for her blessings. And decided that now was as good a time as any. She could go to the little church on Broussard and then take the car on for some shopping, maybe stop by *Anatole's* for lunch.

The decision made, she began to dress. Something simple – for the church – but suitably elegant for the restaurant. The new Calvin Klein suit would be ideal, and she hadn't worn it yet. She fetched the outfit from the wardrobe and laid it on the bed. Plain black shoes with it: the courts from Rayne, she decided. And the pale blue Ralph Lauren blouse; that would complement the darker blue of the suit. Having made her choices, she dressed with typically swift economy of movement. A single, albeit large, pearl on a gold pendant chain set off the sophisticated simplicity of the suit, and she dabbed Givenchy on her throat and wrists. Her purse – Frank had bought it from Ferragamo the last time he was in Italy – completed the ensemble and she paused for a final check in the mirror, pleased with the result.

She had already taken her first pills of the day, but she dropped two more into a little gold pillbox just in case. Like boyscouts, Bryn Mawr girls went prepared.

Leaving the bedroom, she went down the long flight of stairs to the hall. Barry Manilow's voice echoed from the kitchen, and when she opened the door Beatrice, the maid, looked up from the dishwasher and motioned for Joseph, the chauffeur, to reduce the volume. Joseph turned the knob, dulling the sound.

'I'd like the car brought round,' she said.

And Joseph smiled, buttoning the coat of his uniform. She went back into the hall and opened the front door, enjoying the warmth of the Indian Summer as she waited for the Mercedes to arrive. It came with a soft purr and a slight scudding of gravel as Joseph braked. He climbed out, opening the rear door. The interior of the vehicle smelled of leather, and for some reason that offended her nostrils. Usually she loved the smell, but today it seemed to creep up into her sinuses to produce an unpleasant prickling sensation that threatened to turn into a headache. She pressed a button, retracting the left-side window, then told Joseph to drive to the church. The Mercedes growled as the black man went down the drive and past the big bluestone gates onto the road. The flow of air had no effect on her head, even though she realized the leathery smell was reduced now to a faint redolence. Indeed, the pain was becoming a reality, the headache forming at a point directly between her eyes as the throbbing in her sinuses got worse. She located a couple of Excedrin in her purse and swallowed them dry, gagging on the bitter taste. Joseph glanced in his mirror and asked if she was well; she nodded without speaking, waving a manicured hand in indication that he should continue.

By the time they reached the church on Broussard the headache was worse and there was a pain starting up in her stomach. So far it was nothing more than a warning of nausea to come: she was glad she had thought to drop the pills into her purse. She glanced at the Piaget on her wrist and decided it was too early for more pills. An hour's prayer and quiet contemplation should help her overcome the discomfort, and then she could take the gelatine capsules with some food. She looked up as the automobile glided to a halt before the church and Joseph climbed out to open her door. The portico looked inviting; cool and calm and reassuring. Her parents had both been Catholics, and although she did not consider herself an ideal daughter of the Church, she had always maintained a reasonably strict observance of its rituals.

She went inside, feeling as she always did, the sudden tranquillity the House of God offered. The place was empty, light streaming through the ornate stained glass windows to bathe the altar in multi-coloured radiance. She genuflected, dipping her right hand in the small font by the inner door. In the silence, her footsteps rang loud on the flagstones as she walked down the aisle to take a place in the frontmost row of pews. She went down on her knees, surprised when the movement brought a stab of pain to her belly, then ignored it as she began to offer a prayer of thanks.

The pain got suddenly worse, as though in the cool quiet of the church the very tranquillity she so much enjoyed served to emphasize the nausea. She mouthed the prayer instinctively, then opened her eyes and rubbed gently at her midriff. That served only to accentuate the pain and she shifted position. Again, the movement increased the discomfort, sending a sudden, fierce shaft through her intestines. She blinked as her eyes watered, lips clamping hard together, the prayer forgotten. She eased back onto the pew, feeling the polished wood strike cold through the thin material of her clothing. The coolness produced an effect similar to the transition from sauna to cold plunge, goosing her flesh so that she shivered, doubling over as the pain inside her got stronger.

For a while she remained like that, crouched over in the pew with her body trembling. She told herself she was being stupid. The Excedrin were reacting in some way with the prescribed medicines; mental note: no more Excedrin. Then she told herself there was nothing stupid about feeling pain. Stupid was ignoring it. She forced her body to sit upright and folded her hands in an attitude of prayer. This time she prayed for the pain to go away. And then she wondered if that was a selfish prayer, that perhaps she should accept the pain as part of the natural, God-given process of childbirth. She forced herself to concentrate on giving thanks, hoping as she did it that sheer concentration would take her mind off the mounting pressure in her abdomen. When she opened her eyes again, the altar seemed to waver before her. The sunlight reflecting off the huge golden figure of Christ on the Cross struck vicious sparks against her eyes that seemed to combine with the pain in her sinuses to travel on into her brain before linking with the nausea in her belly. It was a drumbeat throbbing now, counterpointed by the gut-wrenching stabs of nausea emanating from her stomach. She swallowed, then gagged, horrified by the abrupt realization that she might be about to vomit.

In seconds the fear became a reality. The roiling in her belly was pushing a hot column of bile up her throat, and she blushed at the thought of fouling God's house. Propriety overcame pain and she climbed awkwardly to her feet, praying now that she could make it to the door before the impending attack disgraced her. She moved along the pews, clutching at the backrests to support herself. Her vision was blurred with tears and her steps were unsteady. She realized that she had not felt this way since she was a sophomore, getting drunk for the first and last time in her life. Once had been enough. And never couldn't be too soon for this unpleasantness to abate.

She got halfway down the aisle before the pain got bad enough she couldn't walk another step. She reached for a pew, but before she could sit down the bile damming up against her clenched teeth began to choke her. Her outthrust hand missed the pew and she went down heavily on her knees, scraping skin against the flags as her head spun and her mouth opened in involuntary release. Tears of shame and pain ran down her face as her stomach emptied. The vomit splashed over her hands, splattering her skirt, the coat, the thin silk of her blouse. It was like fire in her throat, searing her so that for long moments she crouched there, incapable of halting the stream pouring from her opened lips. Then the pain in her belly took on new life, as though, like kerosene poured on a smouldering fire, the bile stoked the furnace of agony centred inside her body. She moaned, spitting vomit, and shook her head. Her eyes caught the sunlit figure overlooking the altar and she turned instinctively for help. She pushed to her feet, her purse forgotten as she staggered down the aisle, wiping vomit from her lips. Each step brought a fresh tremor of agony from her belly and she moved with a constant moaning coming from her mouth, her steps short; jerky. She was close to the rail surrounding the altar before the pain burst inside her and she began to double over again, losing her balance as she went so that she pitched full length on the floor. Her chin struck the hard stone, snapping her teeth together, cutting her lower lip. She tasted blood and began to vomit afresh, ignoring it as the tearing inside her curled her into a foetal ball that knew nothing except pain.

How long she lay there, she could not tell. She felt only agony and a great desire to reach the altar. There she might find solace. Find peace from this suffering. She writhed, not daring uncoil herself from the protective curve in which she sought to cushion her stomach, and wriggled closer to the railing. One outflung hand struck the bars and she pushed open the gate, gritting her teeth as she wormed over the slight steps. She was close enough now to catch the after-scent of incense, but no smell penetrated her nostrils save for the acrid stench of her own puking.

She touched the altar and forced herself to a kneeling position, fingers dug deep into the gold cloth covering the obelisk. There was no longer any definable source for the pain. Rather, it was all over her; all through her; a part of her. She did not know that she was screaming. Nor that her screams were prayers. Nor that they were barely audible. She knew only pain.

It went on and on, a rising crescendo of agony that consumed her, occupying her body with a totality that blocked out all other thoughts. Her hands held tight to the altar cloth as she slid back, dragging the brocade with her, staining it with her vomit. 'Oh, God,' she moaned, golden light burning bright across her vision. And then it was gone in a great surge of red that seemed to boil up from somewhere deep inside her and flood through her, taking away all other sensations, all other thoughts, all other knowledge. She was no longer aware of her position or location, only of the agony. And the single desire that it should go away.

Joseph glanced at the figures showing on the Mercedes' control console: 11.48. Mrs Vansittart had gone into the church at exactly 10.51, saying she would be an hour. Joseph turned back to the paperback he was reading. Things were starting to happen at the Overlook. King was building up to a real big climax.

When he glanced at the clock again, it was 11.57. So the boss lady was taking her time: fine, that gave him longer with Stephen King.

By five minutes after noon Joseph was getting worried. It wasn't like Mrs Vansittart to fall this far behind schedule and he began to wonder if he should put his head around the door. He didn't particularly want to because he didn't want to disturb her at her prayers. Nor did he feel comfortable in Catholic churches – raised on Louisiana revivalist meetings, he always felt something of a usurper inside the more formal places of worship.

When the clock read 12.15, however, he decided he'd better do something. Reluctantly, he closed *The Shining* and stowed the book in the glove compartment. Then he checked the set of his cap and climbed out of the big automobile. He left the door unlocked as he went up the steps to the entrance of the church and pushed in through the big wood doors. It was quiet inside, the air cool, scented with the odours of devotion. The negro paused, letting his eyes adjust to the light. The church was mostly dim, stone pillars shading the hindmost parts, the chancel aglow with light from the windows.

The light was strong enough that he could not make out clearly the shape of the altar. Nor could he see Mrs Vansittart. He cleared his throat, but that brought no response, so he went farther into the long room, removing his cap.

There was a smell intruding on his nostrils now that had nothing to do with churches or worship. Joseph had smelled something like it before, when a fight had started over in Dutch Town. Over a coffee-coloured girl, he remembered. Knives had been drawn and a man had gone down with his belly hacked open. That was a thing Joseph preferred to forget: the man had been screaming as he tried to hold in the entrails bulging from his slashed belly. And the smell had been like this.

He quickened his pace, eyes scanning the pews to either side as he walked nervously down the central aisle. He got closer to the altar and found he could see through the brilliance there. He didn't enjoy what he saw.

79

The woman was on the dais. She had the altar cloth pressed tight against her chest and it was stained with vomit. So was her suit. Her eyes, he could see, were screwed tight shut. Her mouth, in contrast, was wide open, the lips drawn far enough back that her gums were exposed. She was curled up, her knees drawn against her stomach, causing her skirt to ride up. The skirt was soaked with blood. Blood covered her thighs. It was pooled beneath her, trickling sluggishly over the dais to flow down the steps and puddle between the altar and the enclosing railing.

Joseph said, 'Oh, my God,' very softly. Then turned away and began to vomit himself.

When he was done he wiped his mouth and looked around. There was no sign of a priest so he went back outside and lifted the telephone in the Mercedes. A patrol car arrived inside fifteen minutes, disgorging two police-men who listened sceptically to the chauffeur's story, then ordered Joseph to show them the body.

When they saw the dead woman, one of the policemen heaved up his breakfast.

7

Stoner got back to Dallas late on a Saturday morning, reaching his apartment a little after noon. He was not surprised to find Fay waiting for him, but when he moved to kiss her, she drew back, eyes flashing angrily.

'Hey!' Stoner dropped his bag, watching her curiously. 'What's wrong?'

'Why did you lie to me?'

Fay's voice was cold, carrying an edge Stoner hadn't heard before. She stood before the window, sunlight outlining her figure through the chambray blouse she was wearing, hands planted on the hips of her bluejeans. Her gaze was a combination of anger and surprise, as though the source of her irritation came as a shock. Stoner shrugged out of his jacket and tossed the garment over a chair.

'About what?' he asked, feeling an ugly little prickle of guilt.

'Phoenix,' she snapped. 'The funeral of an old friend.'

'Yeah.' Stoner was deliberately evasive. 'What about it?'

Fay stooped to fetch a paper from the low coffee table. And Stoner got a sinking feeling in the pit of his stomach as he saw that the paper was blue, covered with a slanting hand.

'This,' she said, brandishing the letter from his mother like an accusation. 'I came by to clean up a bit and I saw this. I'm sorry I read it – I shouldn't have done that – but I want an explanation.'

'Of what?' Stoner felt suddenly like a man treading water as he wonders where the next wave is coming from. 'What's to explain?'

He wasn't even sure why he was being so evasive. Apart from Fay's desire that he toe Eddison's line, there was no reason he shouldn't have gone to Phoenix, nor anything he couldn't tell her.

Except that he *had* lied about his reasons.

Except that they had planned to use the vacation time to visit Colorado.

Except that for some indefinable reason he couldn't even explain to himself he didn't want to involve her.

'There was no funeral.' Her voice was cold and calm now, the anger verbalizing. 'The old family friend died weeks ago. Was buried weeks ago. Why didn't you tell me, Mike?'

Behind the anger there was a plea, a cry for explanation and reassurance. He said, 'I don't know. I'd better explain.' And it sounded weak even as he said it.

'Go on.' Fay nodded, not moving from her position by the window. She seemed remote. Untouchable. 'I'm listening.'

'Betty was an old friend,' he said, staring at her. 'When I got mom's letter, I thought the circumstances sounded pretty much like Marianne Anders'. I wanted to check it out.'

Fay snorted derisively. 'Are you still on about that? I thought that was done with.'

'No.' Stoner shook his head. 'It's too much of a coincidence. Two wealthy women found dead due to inexplicable haemorrhaging? And it looks like they both attended the same clinic? That's too much. I want to know what's going on.'

'My God!' Fay's hands balled into fists and struck her hips in frustration. 'You've never lied to me before. We always promised there'd be no secrets, and now you're acting crazy because a couple of women have died. We were going away together, Mike. You promised me that. That you'd take this vacation time to visit Colorado. But you went running off to Phoenix instead.'

'I had to.' Stoner shrugged, looking for the right words. Finding them difficult. 'There's something wrong, Fay, and I have to find out what.'

'Why?' she asked bluntly. 'They weren't your patients. There was no evidence of malpractice. So why do you have to find out?'

'I don't know,' was all he could find in reply, 'but I must. Can you understand that?'

'No.' She shook her head. 'Eddison made it clear what would happen if you went nosing around Anders. You're putting your career in jeopardy, Mike. And for what? For some crazy reason you can't even explain properly?'

And it was out in the open now. She was angry that he had lied to her. Angry that they hadn't gone to Colorado. But mostly she was worried about his career. She saw him falling foul of Eddison, getting blackballed at the hospital. Maybe even dismissed. And she was worried that the career she had planned for him would get fouled up. Stoner supposed he should be grateful: after all, her concern was genuine. But he couldn't feel that. The realization that this was mostly about plans he had not agreed to, was scarcely even privy to, hit the hard core of obstinacy that formed an integral part of his character. It was a challenge to his independence; a challenge he had to face, no matter what the consequences.

'I'm sorry,' he said slowly. 'I should have told you why I was going.'

'Would it have made a difference if I'd asked you not to?' Fay demanded. 'If I'd told you I wanted to go to Colorado instead?'

'No.' Stoner shook his head, hating himself for feeling the need to be honest. 'I'd still have gone.'

Fay nodded. Thoughtfully. Taking great care, she folded the letter and set it back on the coffee table. Then she took a deep breath and turned to face him again.

'This is more important than us?'

'No.' Stoner wished he had a drink in his hand. Wished

Fay could understand. Wished he could explain. 'It's not more important than us, but it is important to me. There's no reason it should affect us. Not now.'

'You lied to me. I can't forgive that, Mike.'

The light entering the room from behind her set her face in shadow, but Stoner thought he saw the glisten of tears in her eyes. He took a step forwards, but she lifted a hand as though to ward him off and he halted, an ugly knot of apprehension curdling in the pit of his belly.

'I'm sorry,' he said again. 'The next time I'll tell you. I promise.'

'The next time!' She was genuinely shocked now. 'You're going on with this . . . whatever it is?'

Stoner nodded dumbly. 'I have to, Fay. I can't leave it now. I've got Rafe checking for me – looking for similar cases.'

'God!' Fay folded her arms over her breasts, hugging herself. 'Are you going crazy, Mike? Can't you take Eddison's hints?'

'No,' he said, 'I can't.'

'I think that says it.' Fay picked up a loose-knit sweater. Irrelevantly, Stoner saw that it carried a Nieman Marcus label, watching as she draped it around her shoulders. 'I think it's time you got your priorities sorted out. I'll stay in my apartment until you know what it is you want, Mike. When you've made a choice between me and playing detective, let me know.'

'Fay!' He moved to stop her as she came away from the window, but a barrier had come down and he saw that he could not cross it, so he stood aside. 'There's no call for this.'

'I think there is.' She paused at the door. Stoner saw that the tears were real, and that she looked very lovely. And equally determined. 'I think you need some time to think about what you're doing. To think about us. You do that, Mike. Think about it carefully.'

The door swung shut behind her, the thud of its closing

seeming oddly loud. Stoner took a deep breath and let it out slowly. He crossed to the coffee table and poured himself a stiff Jack Daniels. Added three ice cubes from the thermos bucket. He emptied half the drink on the first swallow, and topped the glass, not adding any ice. There was an air of finality in the room. The full impact of Fay's departure hadn't sunk in yet, and Stoner was reacting in a kind of emotional limbo. He wondered when the full shock would hit. And knew even as he wondered that he could do no more than he was already doing. He was committed to a path, and he would never forgive himself if he failed to follow it up. On that, his mind was made up. He did not want to lose his position at the hospital, nor did he want to lose Fay. But now he was forced to reassess their relationship. He hoped it would not mean an end, but he knew that he could not give up – whatever the hell it was he had gotten himself into.

He was reaching for the bottle again when the telephone rang.

His first thought was that Fay was calling from the lobby, then Rafe Antrim's alcohol-husked voice echoed in his ear.

'Mike? This is Rafe.'

'Yeah, Rafe?' Stoner sipped Jack Daniels. 'What you got?'

'Some kind of pattern, I think.' Antrim sounded excited. 'I want to meet.'

'Sure. When and where?'

Antrim named a bar on Harry Hines Boulevard, and Stoner agreed to meet him there at 6.30. When he put the 'phone down, he was vaguely surprised to realize he was too excited to worry about Fay. He got undressed and took a shower, then pulled on jeans and a shirt and spent the remainder of the afternoon listening to old Dylan albums. Somehow the protest songs seemed to suit his mood.

* * *

The bar was large and dimly lit, crowded at the cocktail hour. Stoner found Antrim holding solitary court in a booth at the far end, his craggy face thrown into stark relief by the single, low-wattage lamp on the table. Antrim had an Old Crow in front of him and a small sheaf of notes. Stoner was surprised to see the drink was scarcely touched, but – he reminded himself – this seemed to be his day for surprises. He fetched a Pabst from the bar and sat down facing Antrim.

'This is some kind of weird,' said the newspaperman. 'I've still got feelers out, but what I've found so far sets my nose to twitchin'.'

He tapped the side of his nose and winked conspiratorially. Stoner was too anxious to hear what he had found to smile at the gesture.

'Thirteen women in the past twelve months so far.' Antrim glanced at his notes, then at Stoner's face. 'Doesn't sound like too many, given the population of the US, but you think about it, Mike.'

Stoner thought about it.

'They're all over,' Antrim continued. 'The one – the Anders woman – right here in Dallas. A second in Dallas. The wife of some bigwig in television. One in Chicago. Your friend in Phoenix. Four in New York. One in Bâton Rouge. Two in Los Angeles, one in San Francisco. One in Denver. There could be any number of others, some we'll find out about, more we'll never hear of.'

Stoner stayed silent as he turned the sheets, waiting for Antrim to go on.

'Like you thought, they were all wealthy. Anders and your girlfriend, we know about. The Manners woman here, her husband is real high up. Keeps an apartment in town and a ranch-house outside. Private aircraft – that kind of wealthy. The woman in Chicago? She was a dyke. Living with a girlfriend on her family money and her alimony. Rich. The woman in San Francisco was married to some film producer. My contact said he's rolling in it. He was also twice her age, which could mean AID. That's a hard part to check – not too many men are going to admit they can't give their wife a baby. But they were all well off, Mike.

'Second point is, they all died the same way and the pattern after that was similar. Mysterious death reported on the local news – small piece in the papers – then nothing. No follow-ups, no explanation. Just a blank. Coupla guys I spoke with said they thought there was something odd about it. But when they tried to follow through, they couldn't get anywhere. Just like you couldn't.'

Stoner said, 'What about the clinic? The Walters Institute?'

Antrim shrugged. 'Not much, Mike. That's maybe not surprising – Hell! unless something happens, a clinic's not news.'

'Dead women are,' said Stoner slowly.

'Yeah.' Antrim nodded and took a sip of his drink. 'Anyway, the Walters Institute is a place up in Oregon. It's way off in the hills back of Portland. Very,' he emphasized the word, 'chic. Very expensive. The kind of place only wealthy people can afford. It's some kind of health place for the most part, but it also handles artificial insemination. There aren't too many operations doing that, and the Walters Institute is considered one of the best, if not *the* best. Exclusive clientele – if that's what you call them – and a very rigorous screening process. Only the cream allowed in.

'A guy called,' he checked his notes again, 'yeah, Ivan Vereker runs it. He's around sixty years old. Specializes in genetics.'

'I've heard of him,' Stoner murmured. 'He published some stuff back in the 70s. Something about foetal control. Some of his techniques are applied now, but I think his stuff was pretty theoretical.'

'Seems like it was good enough to impress the government,' said Antrim. 'The clinic not only makes an undisclosed fortune tending rich ladies, it also collects some healthy government funding. For what, I couldn't find out. Oh, one other thing. All the dead women had above-average IQs.'

Stoner nodded some more. 'So we've got thirteen – maybe more – women dying the same way. All wealthy, all high IQ. We know that two of them visited the Walters Institute. And we know it's the kind of place the others might use.'

'Yeah.' Antrim drank more bourbon. 'And somewhere in there is a story.'

'How do we dig it out?' Stoner asked. 'You're more used to this kind of thing than I am.'

'Shovel the shit off your own doorstep first,' grinned Antrim. 'Lualla Manners was married to Gerald, VP of Station KXW – right here in Dallas. We go to him.'

'If he'll see us,' said Stoner. 'He may clam up like Anders.'

'Then we really wonder if somethin' is afoot,' grunted Antrim. 'And if Manners won't co-operate, then we go to someone else. Keep on going until somewhere down the line someone tells us something. What the hell it'll be, I can't imagine.'

'Um.' Stoner drank Pabst and wiped froth from his lips. 'I wonder.'

'I'll call him tomorrow,' Antrim said. 'Let you know what he says. How's Fay?'

Stoner shrugged. 'Not good, Rafe.'

He explained what had happened and the newspaperman grimaced. 'Sounds kinda like me and Joan. I'm sorry, Mike, but what can I say? I hope you work it out?'

'We will,' Stoner grunted. 'One way or another.'

'You could forget this.' Antrim tapped his notes. 'Leave it to me. That should keep Fay happy.'

'No.' Stoner shook his head. 'I'm in too deep now,

Rafe. If Fay can't handle that, then she can't handle the way I am. I'm not backing out now.'

'That's my boy.' Antrim emptied his glass. 'You want to get drunk? Or you want to come back to my place an' smoke some grass?'

Antrim's apartment was small – a single room with a built-in kitchen and bar, and a small bedroom – and cluttered the way a bachelor's apartment gets cluttered: with a kind of dishevelled organization. He motioned for Stoner to sit down and put some Jerry Jeff Walker on the stereo system. Then he poured two big measures of Jack Daniels and set the bottle on the table between them alongside a big ice bucket. He went to the refrigerator and produced a plastic envelope of marijuana and the fixings. When he had the bomber rolled, he got it lit and passed it to Stoner. The doctor sucked in a deep lungful of the aromatic smoke and held his breath before letting it out in a slow sigh.

After a while it didn't seem to matter that Fay might be leaving him. He could focus his attention only on the problem of the dead women and the mysterious clinic.

By the time they had smoked two joints, they reached the decision that Stoner was too far gone to chance driving, so Antrim layered some sheets over the couch and they settled down to get bombed while Jerry Jeff sang about looking for the heart of Saturday night. Stoner flopped on the couch in a pleasantly euphoric state, letting the grass carry him off to sleep and a highly erotic dream about Fay. He awoke with sunlight on his face and the smell of coffee in his nostrils. Antrim was standing before him holding a cup of steaming black coffee.

'You look like you need this.' He passed the cup to Stoner, then added whisky to his own. 'Want a belt?'

'No.' Stoner shook his head. 'I had enough last night. What time is it?'

'Ten after eight.' Antrim glanced at his watch. 'You got time to make the hospital.'

Stoner swung his legs off the couch and drank coffee. It cleared his head enough that he felt able to stand up and walk into the tiny bathroom. He showered, then used Antrim's Braun on his chin before pulling on last night's clothes.

'You'll call me?' he asked at the door.

'I'll come by tonight,' said the newspaperman. 'What time'll you be home?'

'Around four,' Stoner said.

'I'll be there at 4.30.' Antrim grinned. 'I got the editor's permission to go ahead on this one.'

Stoner felt a slight discomfort at the thought of Antrim mentioning the affair to anyone else. And then dismissed it: like the old Buffalo Springfield song said, Paranoia strikes deep. Rafe had to get his editor's go-ahead to use time checking it out. There was no way around that, so feeling bad about it was just worrying about nothing.

'Great,' he said. 'See you later.'

Antrim watched him go out to the Mustang and drive away, then – still in his undershorts – he took his notes from the filing cabinet set beside his small desk and checked a number. After a while a voice that sent erotic shivers down his spine said, 'Hi there. This is Station KXW, the voice of Dallas. Can we help you?'

'Yeah,' said Antrim, wondering what she looked like, 'I'd like to speak with Gerald Manners. It's important.'

Stoner parked the Mustang in the hospital lot and entered the building from the side. At some point during the day he felt certain he would run into Fay, and he felt nervous about it now that the excitement of Rafe's findings and the effects of the grass had abated. He changed into hospital whites and went looking for something to do.

He got plenty. Almost immediately, he was called in to

help with an emergency – a scaffolder who had missed a vital pin and fallen sixty feet onto concrete as a result. After that, a woman was brought in with a nine inch knife slash opening her left forearm. Another day at Dallas Memorial had begun.

Stoner worked through until the afternoon. The scaffolder was patched up as well as he could be and put in traction. He was still unconscious, hooked up to the life-support machinery with a 20–80 chance of surviving and worse odds on walking again. The woman was sewn up and handed back to the waiting DPD officers, who wanted to ask her how come the same knife that had slashed her arm ended up hilt-deep in the ribs of the man she lived with. Stoner took a shower and went to find himself some coffee and something to eat: Rafe's idea of breakfast was a pot of Red Mountain and a few belts of liquor.

He was grateful to find the cafeteria almost deserted. There was no sign of Fay, nor any mutual acquaintances who might have asked him awkward questions. He felt like forgetting his emotional problems, at least for a few days, until he could – as Fay had suggested – get his priorities sorted out. He didn't want to talk about them, or even think about them. They needed time to coalesce, to shape a firm decision. Hashing them over was no good: he needed to concentrate on something else. Like work, he thought, grinning to himself. Or dead rich women.

Then his buzzer sounded and he was hurrying to an internal 'phone. A few seconds later he was riding the elevator to the ninth floor, where a pregnant woman who already had a weight problem was choking on a hard-centre candy smuggled in to her by a well-intentioned friend.

Like his morning, Stoner's afternoon was busy, and he was glad to climb into the Mustang and head for home, wondering what Rafe would have to tell him. He parked the car and climbed the stairs to his apartment. Once inside, he poured himself a large martini and switched on the afternoon news. The President was talking about limited nuclear war in Europe and Opec was increasing the price of crude oil; Dallas was still enjoying unseasonably warm weather, and the forecast was good: no sign of change. He flicked the set off as a commercial began and found himself wondering what Fay was doing. There was a sudden impulse to call her, but he resisted it, sipping his drink and staring out the window at the sun-brightened skyline. The drink was still in his hand when the doorphone rang at 4.38.

Antrim came into the apartment with an excited look on his face.

'I think maybe we're getting somewhere, Mike.' He went over to the table and helped himself to whisky. Then: 'You all right?'

'Yeah,' Stoner said absently. 'Fine.'

'Hear from Fay?'

Antrim said it casually, but Stoner could sense the concern there. He grinned, not feeling much like it, and shook his head.

'No. Tell me what you found out.'

'It wasn't easy.' Antrim lowered his big frame into a lowslung chair. 'Getting past the secretaries at that place is a damn' sight harder than failing an Army medical, but I used the ole Antrim charm an' got to speak to the man himself. And he says he'll talk to us! Tomorrow, at 3.00.'

'Us?' Stoner's brief attack of lethargy was gone. 'I'm on duty, Rafe.'

'Take time.' Antrim shrugged. 'The man'll only see us together. I came on strong about how his wife wasn't the only one to die like that, an' I was investigating along with a genuine doctor. I think that scared him some – he didn't want to talk about it at first. Tried handing me the bum's rush until I made like I know a lot more than I do. Funny that – you can lead people on, make 'em answer questions, if they just think you may know the answers already. Anyway, I convinced him this wasn't just muck

92

raking, an' we're really taking this seriously, so he said OK. So long as it's 3.00 tomorrow. And you're there, too. I go alone, Manners'll clam up. Believe me, Mike. I know.'

'OK.' Stoner made his decision fast. 'I'll make time. Where do we meet?'

'The Hilton on Commerce.'

'Fine,' Stoner said. 'There anything else?'

'Background mostly.' Antrim freshened his drink. 'This guy is very cool. You know? Big executive, not taking any shit from no reporter. But worried. Worried enough he didn't cut me off, and worried enough he's agreed to talk to us. His wife died six months ago, so I guess he's over the initial shock, but he still doesn't want any dirt dug up. I don't think there's any to dig – she was found in bed in their city apartment and Manners came under suspicion automatically, but he was cleared straight away. I got details of that from a homicide cop I know owes me some favours, guy called Rickenbacker. I mentioned the Walters Institute like I knew that's where they'd gone, and Manners just let it slip that I was right. Seemed like he was pretty uptight, me knowing that.

'I think he's got something to tell us, Mike. And I think that if we can let him believe you're along because there's official medical concern, we'll get a lot farther than I would alone.'

'Don't worry,' Stoner said. 'I'll be along.'

'Yeah.' Antrim nodded, and Stoner sensed that he was worried Fay's influence might dissuade him from pursuing the matter. He emptied his glass and thought about mixing a fresh martini. Decided against it and turned to Antrim with the Jack Daniels in his hand and a question on his face. To his surprise, the newspaperman shook his head.

'I figger it's about time I cut down. I got a feeling about this thing I haven't had for a long, long time: I want to stay on top of it.'

Stoner set the bottle back in place.

'All right. You want to eat?'

'What I want is a drink,' Antrim said, a rueful grin crinkling his features. 'But I need to stay sober to cover this. So . . .'

He spread his hands in an expansive gesture that somehow combined resignation with determination.

'I'll cut down. Maybe just until this is over. Maybe for good.'

'You'll live longer,' Stoner grinned. 'I've told you that often enough.'

'That, my friend,' said Antrim with a sigh, 'is medical advice, and that's something you listen to and forget about if you want. What I got is a gut feeling. That, you don't argue with.'

'So OK,' Stoner laughed. 'Let's go eat.'

8

Gerald Manners met Stoner and Antrim in the lobby of the Hilton, and led the way through to one of the hotel's bars. He was a slender, fit-looking man, around the early forties, Stoner estimated, with prematurely grey hair and an expensive tan. He wore a black suit and a sober tie; whether as a mark of mourning, or because that was how Vice Presidents of television companies dressed, Stoner wasn't sure. He seemed pleasant enough, offering a firm handshake and a measured smile as Antrim made the introductions.

At this time of the day the bar was almost deserted, and they took a booth midway down the room, well away from the few other occupants. Manners ordered a Perrier and Stoner asked for coffee. Antrim took a Holstein. The television executive seemed self-assured as he slid into the booth and sipped the mineral water, smiling expectantly.

'You made this sound extremely urgent.' He adjusted one spotless cuff. 'I can give you 45 minutes, then I have a meeting.'

'We appreciate your giving us the time.' Antrim produced a notepad and a small Pilot roller tip. 'Do you object to my making some notes?'

Manners shook his head. 'But I reserve the right to check them.'

'They're in shorthand.' Antrim grinned, looking almost apologetic.

Manners smiled back. 'That's fine. I read shorthand.'

Antrim's smile faltered for a moment, then he hid his surprise.

'Good. There's no problem then.'

Manners went on smiling calmly; waiting.

'About your wife,' Antrim began, but the executive raised a hand, gesturing for him to stop.

'Let's not waste time with established details, Mister Antrim. I've no doubt you've read the police reports on Lualla's death – so you know that she was found dead in our apartment from massive blood loss due to extreme internal haemorrhaging. You mentioned the Walters Institute, so you've no doubt put two and two together and come up with the answer that Lualla was pregnant by artificial means. Ergo, I am sterile.'

Antrim nodded and Stoner grinned, deciding that he could like Gerald Manners.

'I am,' continued the grey-haired man. 'It's not something I broadcast. Nor a thing I should like broadcast.' He glanced at both men; Antrim shook his head. 'For what it's worth, I was wounded in Viet Nam. I got mortar fragments in my abdomen and when the doctors had dug them all out, they told me I was sterile. I've come to terms with that.' He smiled again. 'Indeed, in some circumstances it's an advantage. I am not impotent, you see. Merely incapable of fathering children. Lualla and I discussed the matter at great length and decided that artificial insemination was the answer. We chose the Walters Institute because we heard it's the best.'

'But your wife died,' Antrim said softly.

Manners' smile left him, and for an instant, it seemed that his face lost its tan, matching the silvery shade of his hair. Then he was in command again, his composure regained.

'Yes,' he said sombrely. 'Lualla died. Inexplicably, Mister Antrim. There was no obvious cause for the haemorrhaging. She had been complaining of some nausea, but nothing really serious. She had the finest medical care available, but she still died. And no one could tell me why. Is that why you're here, Doctor?'

The abrupt swing of direction took Stoner by surprise. Manners was staring at him, and he noticed for the first time that the man's eyes were unusually pale. Almost silvery. They were eyes that demanded immediate answers.

'Yes,' he said quickly. 'There are similar incidents reported all over the country. Women dying the same way.'

'And there's an official enquiry?' Manners' question was direct: it put Stoner neatly on a spot the doctor didn't enjoy. He was faced with a choice: lie to the man and hope he could cover his tracks, or tell him the truth and hope he would go along with it. Something about Manners' attitude prompted Stoner to take a chance.

'Not official,' he said warily. 'A woman died here recently. Marianne Anders.'

'I knew her,' Manners murmured. 'Larry did some work for me.'

'So maybe you know how she died,' Stoner continued. 'Bled to death behind the wheel of a runaway Porsche. And the autopsy showed nothing. And there was no follow-up – Anders had her cremated.'

'He was upset,' Manners said. 'As I was. You can appreciate our feelings. So what – exactly – is your status?'

'Strictly amateur.' Stoner stared directly at the pale blue eyes. 'I was warned off pursuing the matter, but a childhood friend – in Phoenix – died the same way. Rafe here checked his contacts and came up with thirteen women during the past twelve months. All of them wealthy, and all with a high IQ. Two at least attended the Walters Institute. Betty Ramsden, I know for sure did. Marianne Anders had a card in her purse.'

'She attended.' Manners nodded. 'It was she told Lualla about the place. Are you suggesting the Institute is responsible?'

'I'm not suggesting anything,' Stoner replied. 'I'm trying to make what looks like a series of unrelated incidents form some kind of pattern. I want to know why thirteen women have died.'

'Unofficially.'

'Unofficially. I shouldn't be here now.'

Manners steepled his fingers and stared for a moment at the neatly filed nails.

'Why are you telling me all this, Stoner? Aren't you afraid I'll clam up?'

'Yes,' said Stoner honestly. 'Laurence Anders did just that. But someone has to talk, Mister Manners. Sooner or later. Someone will want to know why their wife died – if there's the chance it was something could have been prevented. Or could be prevented in the future.'

'Altruistic.' It was impossible to tell whether Manners meant it sarcastically.

Stoner shrugged. 'Maybe. I'd call it being a good doctor. I was taught that caring for people is the first step. I'm curious, too. But I'd like to know what's causing the deaths so someone can maybe do something about it.'

Manners nodded solemnly and turned to Antrim.

'And your interest is the story?'

'Sure.' Antrim nodded in turn. 'Something's goin' on. I can smell a story.'

Manners sipped Perrier water, suddenly distant from his companions. He set the glass down neatly on the coaster and said, 'Very well. I'll answer any questions I can. With one provision.'

Stoner and Antrim studied his impassive face. The newspaperman took a sip of his beer. Glanced at Stoner, who shrugged and nodded, then said: 'OK. We'll take it.'

'You keep me informed,' said Manners. 'If there's the slightest chance that Lualla died because – what? – there was some kind of foul play, I want to know about it. Effectively, I wish to become a member of your unofficial investigation. I am a wealthy man and I am able to command considerable resources, so I could be extremely useful. Agreed?'

Stoner said, 'Sure,' before Antrim looked at him. His words were echoed by the newspaperman's agreement.

'Excellent.' Manners laid his hands flat on the table. Stoner noticed that he wore a solid gold Rolex. The gleam matched the colour of the links on his French cuffs. 'Ask your questions.'

Antrim took over again.

'Tell us about the Walters Institute.'

'Exclusive. Luxurious. Expensive. Its reputation is impeccable. Wealthy people go there because they're the only ones who can afford it. The place is set in some truly lovely country in the hills behind Portland. The place operates as a health clinic – you can diet up or down, take treatments. I'm sure you know the kind of thing.

'The AID side is separate and discreet. The guests – or was Lualla a patient? – mingle. Ostensibly, you're there to take a cure, so no one is embarrassed.'

As Stoner listened to the firm voice he got the feeling that Manners didn't often feel embarrassment.

'They are very particular about whom they accept. I was impressed by that. It's far from a question of booking your time and paying your bill – they carry out detailed investigations of all applicants. I'd imagine you've discovered that; or suspected it. Whatever, there's a check on physical fitness; psychological tests; even a kind of means test, but in reverse.'

'Hence only wealthy women with above-average IQ,' Antrim murmured.

'And all around thirty,' added Stoner.

'Lualla was twenty-eight,' said Manners. 'Who were the others?'

Antrim consulted his notes and read out the names. Manners nodded twice: 'I know they attended. I didn't know they'd died.'

His voice was lower now, and there was the sparkle of something that might have been either interest or fear or anger in his eyes. He folded his hands together, resting his chin as he stared into the distance curtailed by the bar's farther wall.

'Did you meet Ivan Vereker?' Antrim asked.

'Once. Lualla was attended by a man called Wyeth, but we both met Vereker for the final interview. You're not suggesting he's some kind of mad scientist, are you?'

'No.' Antrim shook his head. 'But it's his clinic. And now we know that at least four of the dead women went there.'

Manners looked down at his glass. The ice was melted now and the Perrier was flat, the lime slice floating in the still water like a drowned corpse.

'Presumably you contacted the Institute when your wife died,' prompted Antrim.

'Of course.' Manners looked up, a slight cording drawing in his cheeks. 'I spoke with Wyeth. He was suitably sympathetic. Sent a wreath. He talked about foetal incompatibility and offered any assistance. I told the coroner, but I don't know if he followed it up. I suppose not, if he was satisfied with his findings.'

'Foetal incompatibility doesn't kill.' Stoner's voice was low, confused. 'The womb may reject the seed, or it may reject the foetus later, but that doesn't kill. That doesn't cause massive haemorrhage. Some blood loss, perhaps. But not this way.'

'You're saying that Wyeth lied?' Manners asked.

'I don't know,' said Stoner. 'All I know is that there's still no explanation.'

Manners' knuckles whitened as his hands tightened. 'There's a pretty big implication in there.'

'I know.' Stoner nodded. 'I'm not sure where we're heading, but the direction right now looks like Oregon.'

'Was anything else said?' Antrim asked.

Manners shrugged. 'Not really. Wyeth made placatory noises. He was anxious there shouldn't be any adverse publicity.'

'He asked you to keep it quiet?' Antrim leant forward across the table, his Holstein forgotten.

'Not like that,' murmured Manners, 'but I suppose you

could say that was the gist of it. The good name of the Institute, all its research lost because of a single unfortunate incident – that kind of thing.'

'And the coroner said nothing more?'

'Nothing,' Manners confirmed. 'I've had relatively little experience of death, so I tended to assume that was the norm. A busy office, that kind of thing.'

'It may be nothing,' Antrim said, 'but none of these deaths got followed up. It's almost as if there's a big hush job operating.'

'Surely that's understandable,' Manners argued. 'In my own case, I saw no reason to prolong the grief. Lualla was dead and I had to come to terms with that. I imagine that few men would want the knowledge they were sterile made public.'

'Yeah.' Antrim chewed on the end of his Pilot. 'That could be a reason. But I wonder how many got a similar spiel from this Institute.'

'I really don't know.' Manners glanced at his watch. 'I've told you all I know. What do we do next?'

Stoner heard the *we* and felt a rush of relief. If Manners was as well-connected as he claimed, he could be a useful ally.

'We got a choice,' said Antrim. 'We can try talking to some more husbands, or we can check out the Walters Institute.'

'You're the journalist,' Manners said. 'You tell us.'

'Newspaperman,' Antrim corrected automatically. 'I'm a newspaperman. And I don't think we'll get too much mileage out of the husbands. Either they'll refuse to talk, or they won't know any more than you do. I say we go for the Institute.'

'How?' Stoner asked.

'Legwork,' grunted Antrim. 'I'll fly up to Portland and take a look around.'

'Will they agree?' Manners asked.

'I think so,' said Antrim. 'I'll come on like I'm doing a

feature on commercial medicine. They should buy that. No reason why not, if they've nothing to hide.'

Manners nodded. 'When will you go?'

'Soon as I clear it with my editor.'

Manners reached inside his coat to produce a leather wallet. He took out a card and passed it to Antrim, then handed one to Stoner. The cards were heavy and richly grained, black lettering on the white read simply, *Gerald Manners* above two telephone numbers, one preceded by the single word, *Home*, the second by *Office*.

'That's a private line.' He folded the wallet and dropped it back inside his coat. 'The home number is my apartment. I spend more time there than at the ranch just now. The ranch is in the book.'

Stoner and Antrim put the cards away.

Manners said, 'If you have difficulties with your editor, let me know. I can probably square it.' He glanced at the Rolex again: 'And now I have to go. Let me know what happens.'

Antrim shook hands, then Stoner. They watched as the television executive strode down to the bar, where a young man with a button-down collar and a worried expression was talking with a group of smiling Japanese. Manners strolled up and took the party away.

'I think we're gettin' somewhere,' grinned Antrim. 'This guy could be useful.'

'Yeah.' Stoner nodded, sipping cold coffee.

He felt like a man confronted for the first time with one of those executive puzzles. A Rubik cube, or something like that. There were all the bits, all the colours, staring up at you. All you need do is twist them around some until they make the right pattern. But twisting them the right way is not quite so simple. He had facts, sure. Big, ugly facts like death. Or like what could be a hush job. Or like, why did the Walters Institute keep cropping up? But all those pieces were still in need of the twist that would drop them into the final design. The Walters Institute seemed to be the random factor now, but he couldn't see how a respectable – indeed, a government funded – clinic would, or could, get itself mixed up in – what? He had to admit that he didn't right now know what the hell it was the Institute might, or might not, be mixed up in. All he knew for sure was that there was something, and that he intended to find out what that *something* was.

'You gonna sit there brooding the rest of the day?' Antrim interrupted his musings. 'Or we gonna have another drink?'

Stoner glanced at his own watch.

'What the hell? Let's have a drink.'

They went up to the bar and Antrim called for a second Holstein, while Stoner asked for a Bloody Mary.

'Not bad.' Antrim studied his glass. 'Not bad at all.'

'What's not?' Stoner asked, frowning.

'Two beers,' grinned Antrim. 'All I've had today. That's fucking good, now I come to think of it.'

'That's fantastic,' Stoner grunted. 'When you going to Oregon?'

'I'll talk to Holmes this afternoon.' Antrim sucked beer with an appreciative sigh. 'If there's no fuss, I'll square it with the Institute and fly up soon as I can. Maybe tomorrow. I'll call you later – let you know when I'm going.'

'Right.' Stoner drank the Bloody Mary. 'You doing anything tonight?'

'Nothing special.' Antrim shrugged. 'You feeling lonely?'

'Something like that.' Stoner wiped tomato juice from his upper lip.

'Call her,' said Antrim.

'No.' Stoner shook his head. 'Not yet. There's no point yet.'

9

She was humming. She always hummed because aircraft made her nervous and the drone of sound she kept up in her head helped keep the fear at bay. It didn't matter how many statistics Eddy quoted at her, or how many times she'd flown before, the fear remained a constant. It was a fact of her life, and she accepted it as such in the same way she accepted the need to take a sleeping pill or, at Thanksgiving, to entertain Eddy's hideously boring relatives. It was simply there, to be borne until it went away; which meant when the aircraft was safely on the ground again and she was inside the terminal building. Until then she would hum, a little more loudly on take-off and landing, more softly during flight, even breaking off if the person in the next seat managed to start up a conversation.

Often as not, the person in the next seat was a man, and he would start talking. After all, she was an attractive woman. Her thirtieth birthday had passed four days ago (Eddy had presented her with a Piaget so damn' thick with diamonds she found it hard to tell the time, and then took her outside to where a De Lorean was waiting with a big red bow around the gullwing doors) and she knew she looked closer to twenty-five. Her figure was good: careful dieting and plenty of exercise kept it trim. She dressed well – should on the allowance Eddy gave her – knowing that a wardrobe out of Klein and Halston and Lauren helped a girl to improve on what nature had given her. And her make-up was calculated to emphasize the best features of her face, which were her eyes and mouth. She had been a model before she met Eddy three years ago, and married him after a whirlwind courtship that saw him jetting in to visit her on location in Mexico and Argentina and, once (to her amazement) Australia. He had pursued her with the singleminded determination he gave to his many business enterprises and after three months of the full jet set treatment, she had accepted his proposal. He was rich – she wasn't sure quite how rich, but *immensely* seemed to cover it; and, to pile perfection on perfection, he was only thirty-two, exceedingly handsome, and utterly charming. She had gone into the marriage with a certain amount of cynicism, expecting them both to have affairs, or maybe break up, within a couple of years, but so far she had been proven wrong. Eddy – she was sure – remained absolutely faithful to her, and she in turn had discovered she wasn't interested in any other men. So when a fellow traveller started a line, she smiled, accepting his compliments, and let the humming drone on inside her mind.

Now, however, she was sitting alone, next to the window. She was humming an old Joan Baez song, *Farewell, Angelina*, staring out the window at the heat haze shimmering around the nozzle of the engine she could see, feeling the vibration of the big turbos shake the body of the aircraft the way her body would be trembling if she wasn't humming. She had taken her seat as early as possible, not wanting to wait around the airport buildings because she knew she'd have a couple of drinks to calm her nerves and drinking maybe wasn't a good idea on top of the capsules.

She had been taking more of the capsules lately because the pangs had gotten worse. They had said that was a possibility – Unlikely, Mrs Scharff, and nothing to worry about – but she wasn't to take more than eight a day, and she was on the limit now. When she told Eddy, he had got worried. And then, in typical no-nonsense style, he had gone ahead and arranged for her to fly up to Oregon for a check-up. Just presented her with instructions and her flight tickets and told her he was sorry he couldn't go with her, but he had to be in Rio de Janeiro for a few days, and there was a car would be waiting for her, and call him when she arrived. So here she was, all dressed up and no one to talk to. Nervous as hell, but maybe that wasn't such a bad thing because at least it took her mind off her stomach. And that had been doing funny things lately.

She smoothed the silver-grey leather of her Halston jacket across her knees, feeling the bulge of a cigarette pack and longing for a smoke, and crossed her trousered legs. She glanced at the Piaget, not sure when they were due to take off. Soon, she hoped, because she thought that before very long she would need the rest room. At least it wasn't far away: Eddy always travelled at the rear of the aircraft. He said there was a better chance of surviving a crash if you were in the tail section, and the hell with first class; so she was, at least, close to the little room.

And then the pilot's voice crackled over the intercom and the aircraft lurched forwards, the turbos rising in pitch as they wheeled around the hardstand and began to taxi towards the runway. The 'plane halted there and the stewardesses went scurrying for their seats, then it was moving forwards, the engines screaming, and there was that awful, pit-of-the-stomach feeling as all that metal hurled itself into the sky.

That was always the worst part. Worse than landing, infinitely worse than the almost-but-not-quite tranquil routine of the flight itself. That was the moment her humming became audible and her stomach threatened to climb up her throat and leave her embarrassed. She closed her eyes, trying to make herself concentrate on the words . . .

Farewell, Angelina, the bells of the town . . . What was the next line? . . . *Have been stolen by bandits, and I must go down* . . .

She wished she was down. She wished she was on the ground. She wished she didn't feel so nervous. She wished she didn't feel so sick.

Not really thinking, she fetched the brown bag from the holder on the seat in front and sat with it clutched in her hands. Just in case.

The aircraft was climbing now, seeming to rise almost vertically as it gained height. The angle of climb and the pressure of the ascent weighed heavy on her stomach and she thought she would need the brown bag if the pilot didn't level off soon. She forgot the words of the Baez song and switched to a Dr Hook number . . .

I could be on a shiny, silver 'plane,
Heading into Denver,
Or slowly floating down to Biscayne Bay . . .

But shiny, silver 'planes were always overheated, so warm you could smell the plastic. She always got a headache when she flew, and this time was no exception: there was a real humdinger building up behind her eyes. She reached up to adjust the airflow from the nozzle above her, but that seemed only to ruffle her hair, rather than cool her, and it did nothing to alleviate the growing headache. She felt her stomach heave again as the aircraft levelled out and sunlight streamed in through the windows across the aisle. The warning lights went off and she fumbled in her Lou Taylor purse for the little gold Dunhill Eddy had given her one night in the Bahamas. She found the lighter and tugged a Marlboro from her jacket. It took her a while to get the cigarette lit because her hands were shaking, and when she sucked in the first lungful of smoke, she began to cough. That in itself was unusual: she didn't smoke often, certainly not enough to get coughing fits. But this one wouldn't stop. She felt like she was choking on the smoke, and each harsh cough sent a dull throb of pain through her head.

A stewardess appeared in the seat beside her, a plastic mug of water offered consolingly. The girl eyed her clothes and smiled sympathetically, massaging her shoulderblades as the coughing fit doubled her over.

Finally she got it under control, leaning back in the seat

with her mouth open, breathing shallow for fear of starting it off again. The stewardess took the Marlboro from her hand and stubbed it. As though making some solemn exchange, she took the water and began to sip. It was cold, soothing her throat, and she smiled as she passed the mug back.

'I'm sorry.' She began to rummage in her purse, looking for her compact. 'I'm not usually so awful.'

The stewardess made the kind of noises she must have made to hundreds of nervy passengers and eased away, swaying down the aisle on the look out for other flight-wary travellers. The woman opened her compact and made adjustments to her face. Then she closed her eyes and went on humming, wishing the headache would go away.

It didn't. Instead, it was joined by a nauseous aching inside her. The source was impossible to define; it wasn't coming from any particular part of her body, and she couldn't localize it. It was just there and spreading. And impossible to ignore. The hell with instructions, she decided, there should be a wide enough safety margin she could swallow a couple more of the capsules without ill-effects. And she could call the Institute when she landed if necessary. Though it shouldn't be, because Eddy had a car arranged and she would be there inside a couple of hours. She reached up again and pressed the *Call* button.

The same stewardess materialized beside her, pretty face worried.

'I'd like a glass of water.' She opened her hand to show the pills. 'I'm afraid I don't feel too good.'

'I'll fetch you one.' The stewardess smiled professionally. 'Please use the bag if you need to.'

She nodded, smiling through the growing pain, and clutched the armrests. She was surprised when a new pain lanced through her discomfort and she realized she was grinding her right palm against the ashtray. She put her hands together, rubbing at the sore spot, and noticed that her palms were slick with sweat. Then she realized her face was sheened with perspiration, and the Klein blouse was beginning to feel distinctly tacky. The stewardess came back and she palmed the capsules into her mouth and swallowed them down, gasping as the cold water hit her stomach and set it to cramping. The stewardess got a worried look again, but this time the woman was too wrapped up in her own suffering to worry about anything else. She squeezed her eyes tight shut and tried to force the pain away. It wouldn't go, and after a while she looked up again and licked her lips.

The stewardess said, 'How do you feel? Are you taking anything?'

She replied, 'I feel rotten. I'm pregnant. The pills are for nausea.'

The stewardess nodded understandingly, professional gaze taking in the still-slim figure and deciding there was little chance of an in-flight birth.

'I'll be all right,' she said. 'Really. It'll pass. It always has.'

'You've had this before?' The stewardess sounded grateful.

'Yes.' She nodded, then regretted the movement. 'A few times. It's a little worse right now, but that's probably nerves.'

'Probably.' The stewardess got back on her feet, flicking off the *Call* sign. 'If you need anything else . . .'

She nodded again, forgetting it would hurt, and watched the girl walk away, feeling embarrassed despite herself when the stewardess whispered with another and both heads turned in her direction. That *was* it, she told herself. Just a combination of expected nausea and nerves. Take one pregnant woman, shake well in an aircraft with plenty of nerves added, and there you are: an in-flight cocktail. She laughed weakly and stared at the brown bag, dull against the sheen of her jacket. Not that, she thought, I'm not using that. If I am sick, I shall retire to the rest room and be ladylike about it. And the way I'm feeling, I may be ladylike pretty damn' soon.

She looked out the window at the cottonwool floating past. Damn it! The nausea would pass off soon. The headache would go once she landed. And pregnant women expected some discomfort – that was only natural. Everything about her pregnancy was going to be natural. Now. Not at first, of course. It hadn't been possible to handle that part of it naturally because Eddy couldn't. It was a shock to them both to find that out. God knew, they tried hard enough, because they both wanted children, but nothing had happened. And then the physicals had come up negative on Eddy, and they had been forced to face the fact he was sterile. He had made a joke of it, laughing that he could have saved a lot of money and more worry if only he'd known. Then he had become depressed for a month, snapping out of it when he discovered what he had announced as the perfect solution. He had heard – which meant he had checked very carefully – that there was a place in Oregon handled this kind of thing. Very discreetly. No need for concern about anything. Except, of course, whether or not she wanted to have a child by artificial means. The initial interviews with the people at the Walters Institute had helped convince her. Those, added to Eddy's eagerness, had persuaded her and she had agreed with a minimum of reservations.

The actual process of fertilization had been surprisingly – and pleasantly – brief. There was no discomfort, nor – after lengthy talks with a psychoanalyst called Harlan – any psychological hang-ups. She had settled easily into the pregnancy, and Eddy had been overjoyed; the original proud father. They hadn't told anyone yet, not wanting to break the news until it was unavoidable, which – the way she was keeping her figure – wouldn't be for a month or two. Unless the nausea got worse. Like it had one night at Maude Grover's when she had locked herself in the bathroom and spent thirty minutes losing Maude's excellent dinner. That incident had sparked Eddy's concern, and a repeat performance at the State Fair had convinced him that she needed special treatment. So here she was, feeling lousy on a 'plane on top of her nerves.

But it was worth it.

It had to be worth it.

Didn't it?

A spasm, fiercer than before, caused her to suck in breath, and she doubled over, fumbling to release the safety belt. The Halston jacket slid unnoticed to the floor. The brown bag crumpled as her hands tightened in unconscious reflex. This was bad. Her head was pounding like the Dallas Cowboys were working out inside her skull and there was a kind of wave motion of pain deep within her, washing out from a central core that was burning up her intestines. She let the brown bag drop and pulled a Kleenex from the Lou Taylor, pressing the tissue to her face and feeling it moisten under her hands. God knew what she was doing to her make-up – she'd need to fix it – but her face felt like it was on fire. Come to that, she felt as though she was burning up inside, the pain swilling around so that it splattered at her throat and threatened to spill out her mouth.

It was imperative now. There was no use in pretending it would go away: she was going to vomit.

She struggled to her feet, body hunched so that she missed the jut of the overhead locker shelf, and stumbled into the aisle. A stewardess – a different girl this time – took her arm as she mumbled something about the rest room, and helped her past the curious faces occupying the last two rows.

'I'll be all right.' She clutched the doorframe for support. 'I just feel a little nauseous.'

Before the stewardess could say anything, she had ducked inside the tiny cubicle and shut the door. The temperature was noticeably lower here, and it set her to shivering, her teeth beginning to chatter as goosebumps started up on her arms and breasts. She looked at the polished metal of the washbasin, gleaming antiseptically bright in the stark light of the fluorescent overhead, then at the lavatory bowl. Puking wasn't much fun wherever you were, so she thought she might as well make herself as comfortable as possible. She flushed the bowl and got down on her knees, clutching the metal rim.

And then she vomited.

It came in a thick, hot spurt that seemed to jet up from her stomach with an acceleration rate to match the aircraft's. There was no heaving, just this wash of sour-tasting bile flooding out her mouth like the faucet was jammed open. How long it lasted, she couldn't tell. Checking the time was the last thing on her mind, and all her concentration was focused on emptying her belly. The vomit splashed into the bowl, filling the confined area with an acrid stench that made her eyes smart through the tears already there. She reached blindly to flush the bowl, not watching as the outpouring of her belly disappeared. She threw up some more and then the pain seemed to abate a little.

Thank God, she thought fervently, the capsules must be starting to work.

She spat dribbles of vomit into the stinking water and flushed the bowl a second time. Then a third. Then she turned on the faucet over the sink and washed out her mouth. Rinsed her face, thinking, To hell with make-up, and patted herself dry.

The stewardess knocked on the door, calling an enquiry.

She opened the door, asking the girl to fetch her purse. The stewardess looked at her doubtfully for a moment, then went to fetch the Lou Taylor. When the woman looked in the mirror, she saw the reason for the girl's concern. Her eyes were red, mascara streaked around them so that thin lines of dark, viscous matter ran down her cheeks. Her lipstick was smudged, and somewhere along the line she had bitten her lower lip hard enough to raise an ugly, blood filled welt. She shook her head, and ran water into the basin, deciding that a complete new start was called for, rather than running repairs.

The stewardess returned, passing her the purse, and she set about fixing the damage.

When she was finished, she felt a little better. Not good, but a little better. The headache was still there and she still felt cold, almost as though she was coming down with a chill, but the pain in her belly was less fierce now. She replaced the make-up, decided she was as good as she was going to look, and went out of the rest room.

'I feel a lot better,' she told the solicitous stewardess. 'Sorry about the fuss.'

The stewardess smiled and watched her go back to her seat, then was called away as a kid at the front of the 'plane began to complain. She sat down and opened a copy of *Vogue*, leafing idly through the pages as the engines droned on and more cottonwool floated past. She looked at her watch, trying to remember how long the flight took. About two hours more, she thought. Not too long, if only the pain would hold off. She tried to read an article about fashionable restaurants in New York, but the thought of food threatened to set her stomach off again, so she turned to a piece on ski holidays. It would be nice to go back to Europe. To spend some time in Kitzbühl or San Anton. Maybe Eddy would agree to their going if the Institute said it was OK. She read about the night life in the resorts, then went on to what the beautiful people were wearing on the slopes and off.

That occupied around thirty minutes, and when she was finished she had to admit the pain was still there. In fact, it was getting bad again, building up to some kind of crescendo. Had she not been afraid that the slightest movement would cause worse hurt, she would have squirmed with embarrassment.

But she didn't get time to squirm. Instead, the pain

became agony that seemed to fill her intestines with fire. It locked burning hands on her heart, making her gasp as her breath shortened, and it seemed to be squeezing her stomach – which must be empty now – hard enough that she was retching. She doubled over, banging her forehead on the seat in front, ignoring the irritable grunt from the disturbed passenger, and started to vomit afresh.

The puke was darker now and she felt total panic as she thought she had torn her stomach lining and was spewing blood. It splashed over the silvery grey leather of her jacket, obscuring the Halston label. Over her Klein slacks. Over her Bottega Veneta pumps. Over the forgotten shape of the crumpled brown bag. She was unaware of the stewardesses – both of them now – helping her to her feet and hurrying her to the rest room. All she knew was the pain. The red waves of agony roaring through her insides, pounding in her head. She slumped over the bowl, moaning as her stomach protested the absence of any further matter to disgorge. She crouched like that for long minutes, her body tensed as her throat seared and the heaving eased off to an uncontrollable shuddering. A stewardess wiped her lips, glancing surreptitiously at the stained tissue before depositing it in the disposal unit, while the other knelt with one arm about her shoulders, murmuring unheard encouragement. The woman groaned, raising her head, and then screamed aloud as a raw fury of pain burst inside her. She tore clear of the stewardess' arm, her hands pressed hard against her midriff, swaying back, then forwards to curl in a foetal ball with her face resting against the plastic flooring. The two stewardesses exchanged worried looks, the one crouched in the doorway of the rest room glancing back down the aircraft, where faces showing concern and sympathy and contempt were turned to study the drama. The other girl reached to touch the woman's shoulder, then drew back as a spasm racked the body.

The woman was shaking, twisted on her side now with

114

her knees drawn up tight against her chest. Her eyes were screwed shut, the skin pulled taut over her fine cheekbones. Her lips were clamped tightly together, a thread of spittle hanging from one corner of her mouth. There was mucus running from her nostrils and she was horribly pale, twin spots of bright red standing out against the pallor where the bones stretched the skin. A dark stain spread across the material of her pants, and the stewardess frowned slightly in shared embarrassment as she realized the woman had lost control of her bowels.

Then she gasped as the woman screamed again, the sound rising to a shrill, nerve grinding pitch before tailing away to a harsh, low moaning. Her body jerked, limbs straightening out so that her head banged against the base of the lavatory bowl while her feet thudded hard against the dividing panelling. The stewardess snatched a towel from the holder unit and wadded it to form a protective cushion between the woman's head and the metal lavatory unit. In the doorway, her companion crouched, shielding the scene from the other passengers with her back, her eyes wide and horrified.

Abruptly as the straightening motion had begun it reversed itself, the woman's body curling again, rolling into a tight, trembling ball.

The stewardess in the doorway said, 'Oh my God!'

And when her companion followed her stare, her face went pale.

Over the floor of the cubicle, smeared by the movement of the woman's body, there was a long, wide slick of liquid. In the glare of the fluorescent lighting it appeared brown, and the stewardess' first thought was that the woman must be suffering some kind of gastric disorder. But there was no smell, not of diarrhoea. Instead, there was a sweetish, cloying odour. And the slick was not brown, but a dark red.

And it grew as the stewardess watched, the stain across the crotch of the woman's pants getting steadily larger, fluid exiting with sufficient force that it was bubbling through the material, seeping into the sodden fabric and spreading. The woman was still groaning, but now the sound was far back in her throat, a feral cry, primal in its hurting. She was straining, legs parting as though she sought to thrust out a child, or sought to expel the agony through the exit point of her vagina. The stewardess unfastened her pants, tugging them down her legs, followed by the wispy silk of her undergarment. Then gagged as the woman thrust afresh and a great, thick spurt of blood gouted from between her legs. It splashed over her thighs and ran sluggishly across the floor. The stewardess stared at her bloodied hands and turned a face that was now genuinely frightened to her companion.

'Tell Mark what's happening. We'll need emergency clearance and an ambulance standing by.'

The other girl jumped to her feet and hurried down the aisle. She was grateful for a chance to get away from the smell.

The remaining stewardess cradled the woman's head for want of any other treatment she could think of, ignoring the nails that dug into her arm as the woman clutched her. The woman's face was very pale now, and her moaning was noticeably quieter, but the spasms were still coming, sending those awful spurts of stinking blood jetting across the cubicle. The floor of the rest room was thick with the stuff now. It was all over the stewardess' legs and skirt, glistening on her arms and discolouring the front of her blouse. It was lapping over the lower edge of the doorway, soaking into the carpet outside. And it was still coming. That was, perhaps, the worst thing: it seemed unending, as though the woman would go on pumping out blood until her body emptied.

Helpless to prevent it, the stewardess lifted to a kneeling position and began to vomit into the bowl.

A hand passed her a towel and a whisky-husky voice asked, 'Anything I can do?'

She looked up to see one of the passengers standing anxiously in the doorway. He was a big man, with a craggy face that somehow matched his slightly crumpled sports coat and loose-knotted tie. Tousled black hair fell onto his forehead and his not-quite-handsome features were concerned and incredibly reassuring.

The stewardess wiped her mouth and went back to the woman.

'Thanks,' she said, 'but I've told the pilot to radio ahead. I don't think there's anything anyone can do until we land.'

The man was about to say something in reply, but the pilot came down the aisle then, apologizing as he pushed past him. He looked at the woman on the floor of the cubicle and his tanned face lost most of its colour.

'Christ! This really is an emergency.' He stared at the stewardess. Then: 'Is there anything you can do?'

The girl shrugged. 'I don't know. She's bleeding and I don't know how to stop it.'

The pilot said, 'I've got an ambulance standing by and we've got immediate clearance. That gives us about forty-five minutes in the air. See what you can do.'

The stewardess nodded and said, 'I'll try, but I don't think she'll make it.'

The pilot said, 'Shit!' and came close to running as he went back to the cockpit.

The man with the craggy face said, 'Look, do you want me to stick around? Or are you better left alone?'

'We can handle it.' The assurance came automatically to the girl's lips, not backed by any real belief. 'Thanks, but please go back to your seat.'

The man shrugged and went back to his seat.

Twenty-seven minutes and fourteen seconds out of Portland International the woman died.

* * *

Rafe Antrim needed a drink badly as he got off the aircraft. He couldn't be certain, but he thought he had seen the reason for his journey, and he didn't like it. That had been ugly. That was no way for anyone to die. He took a deep breath of clean Oregon air and headed for the nearest bar. He ordered an Old Parr because that was the first label he saw and swallowed the whisky neat. Then he called for a second and this time asked the barkeep to add ice. He sat with the drink in his hand, knowing that he needed it. Needed it badly, because all of a sudden the statistics he was carrying in his notebook had become reality, and that was always a little harder to handle than cold facts put down on paper. And in this particular case the reality had come right up and hit him in the face. Or, at least, splashed his shoes: as he left the aircraft he had noticed that he had tracked bloody footprints down the aisle. Yeah, he needed a drink now if he had ever needed one.

But at the same time, he knew it wasn't going to be any good. He could work his way through that bottle of very good Old Parr and that would blur the knowledge a bit, make it a little easier to digest. But after, when he sobered up, the memory would still be there. Like trying to forget Joan in a haze of alcohol. That hadn't worked and nor would this. What he needed now was to stay sober. One hundred goddam per cent sober. All the way from start to finish. Right down the line sober.

But, God! did he ever need a drink more?

He picked up the glass and took a sip. It tasted good – better than the first. He took another sip, savouring the slightly smoky flavour, the whisky coming hot through the cold tang of the ice: good, very good indeed.

And very bad if he was going to get this story.

And there was a moment of revelation in Rafe Antrim's life. It was, he thought later, how born-again Christians must get the message: a sudden, undeniable flash of knowledge. Not logic; not rational. Just *knowing*.

I, he thought – feeling the thought on a gut level, I am an alcoholic. I cannot function without a drink.

And then he thought, Fuck it! I am also a man who used to be a damn' good newspaperman. I can lick booze.

And a feeling of determination and fierce defiance crept in as he thought: I *will* lick booze. I can, and I will. I am going to put this drink down unfinished and I am going to walk over to that telephone and call Mike. I am going to tell him what I've seen and then I am going to hire a car and get out to that goddam Institute and find out what is going on. And if I don't do that right now, I am never going to do it.

Rafe Antrim left his glass of Old Parr on the bar and walked over to the telephone booth. He was surprised at himself. And rather pleased.

10

Antrim's call caught Stoner staring out the window of his apartment at the lights going on all over Dallas as the sun went down. The *Pathétique* was murmuring from the big Leak speakers and Stoner had a glass of Jack Daniels in his hand. He had been thinking about Fay, wondering if he should call, and he started from his reverie as the stridency of the telephone's bell cut into his thoughts. Climbing to his feet, he reduced the sound of the magnificent music and lifted the receiver.

'Mike?' Antrim's voice was strained. 'I just got in. There was one on the 'plane for Chrissakes.'

'One what?' Stoner asked, confused.

'A woman. Jesus, Mike! She was in the john and there was blood all over. It was coming out of her like water from a faucet. Christ! it was the most godawful thing.'

Stoner carried the telephone across the room and killed the Tchaikovsky. He left his drink forgotten by the stereo equipment as he listened to Antrim's hoarse voice.

'She died in the air, Mike. They took her off covered in a blanket and told us not to worry. But I saw her! And, Jesus! it was horrible.' He paused, and Stoner could hear the rasp of his ragged breathing. 'Her name was Karen Scharff. You got that? Karen Scharff, two *f*s at the end. She boarded at Dallas, so she was maybe local. Check it out, Mike. It could be another lead.'

'How?' Stoner asked, wondering if Antrim had been drinking.

'Call Manners,' said the newspaperman. 'If Karen Scharff fits the pattern, then Manners might have known her. See if you can talk to the husband.'

'Yeah, OK.' Stoner jotted the name on a pad. 'You all right, Rafe?'

'Yeah. No.' Antrim chuckled and it was an ugly sound. 'I'm not drinking, if that's what you mean. I think I've kicked it, Mike. I really do. I'm just shook up.'

'That's good,' said Stoner. 'What're you gonna do now?'

'Rent a car an' find a hotel. I'll head out to the Institute tomorrow. Call you soon as I got more news.'

'Yeah, fine.' Stoner was staring at the name on the pad. 'I'll get hold of Manners.'

'Good. I'll call you.'

Antrim put the telephone down and for several seconds Stoner sat holding the dead receiver. Then, like a man taking sudden control of himself, he depressed the rests and punched Gerald Manners' number.

The television executive answered immediately.

'It's Mike Stoner.'

'Mike!' Manners' voice was calm, but Stoner thought he could sense anticipation behind the smoothness. 'How's it going?'

'There's been another.' Stoner took a deep breath, collecting his thoughts. 'A woman died in the same way on Rafe's plane. A woman called Karen Scharff.'

'Karen?' Now Manners' voice was shocked. 'Eddy Scharff's wife?'

'I don't know,' Stoner said. 'Maybe. Rafe said she fitted the pattern.'

'Eddy's the wealthiest man I know.' Manners' voice was calm again, in control. 'I can find out. What should I do?'

Stoner thought for a moment, feeling suddenly way out of his depth. It was as though he had stumbled across some kind of macabre Pandora's Box, but before he could close the damn' thing, he needed to rummage through the contents until he reached the bottom. If he could. And suddenly he wasn't sure how. A train of events had started and now they seemed almost to be running away with him.

He was in too deep to back off, but he wasn't certain how to get through to whatever secret lay behind the deaths.

'Find out if it was her first,' he said slowly. 'Can you do that?'

'I guess.' Manners thought for a moment. 'It may not be easy, but I'll find out. What else?'

'She was flying to Portland. Maybe she was going to the Institute. We need to know. And why.'

'Leave it to me.' Manners sounded a whole lot more confident than Stoner felt. 'I'll call you back.'

After he had rung off, Stoner picked up his drink and went back to the window. He felt a strong desire to call Fay. To tell her what had happened and try to explain his concern. More than anything, he wanted to talk to someone – anyone – sympathetic. He stared at the telephone, then shook his head, tipping the last of his whisky down his throat. What could he tell her? That Rafe was in Portland because they were going ahead, and another woman had died? Fay would tell him to report it to the authorities and leave it to them. And for no reason he could clearly define, Stoner didn't want to do that. What, after all, could he report? That there were now fourteen cases of death by haemorrhage and there might be a link to a perfectly respectable clinic? If he wasn't laughed off, the report would be noted and duly ignored. No, before he started making any of this even vaguely official, he needed more facts.

As for calling Fay, the rift between them needed more than that to heal it. There was a fundamental personality clash that called for a great deal of understanding and discussion before they could hope to come together again. The thought that they might not struck Stoner with less impact than he had expected. What it really added up to, he supposed, was that Fay was conventionally oriented: she was used to money and wanted to continue used to it, which meant her prospective husband pursuing a career, playing the game without making any waves that might jeopardize his career chances. Crudely put, he believed Fay saw medicine as an honourable means of making money. And he saw it as a way to help people. Making money along the way would be nice, he couldn't deny that, any more than he could deny he enjoyed the luxuries a successful career afforded. But his basic motivation remained that belief instilled in his youth by Dave Carter – that medicine is people, and the doctor who forgets that isn't a real doctor any more.

Stoner decided it wouldn't be a good idea to call Fay just yet.

He poured another drink and stood in front of the window, staring at the kaleidoscope of light shining through the darkness. After a while he pulled the drapes and returned the needle to the start of the *Pathétique*. He felt oddly calm, and very excited at the same time.

Two days later he received another call from Antrim.

'It's just like Manners said,' reported the newspaperman, 'very de luxe. They got a whole tract up in the hills, far enough out of Portland it's pretty isolated. The country's rough an' there's only one road into the place. There's a chainlink fence around the whole goddam thing an' you gotta pass a gatehouse to get in. The guys on the gate are heavies. Very discreet. Very polite. But still heavy.

'I spoke to a doctor called Romero – he seems to be some kind of PR flack as well as being a doctor – and he said the security was for the sake of the "guests", he called them. I guess that figgers – I never seen so much money gathered in one place. It's fixed up like a very expensive holiday resort. Private apartments, chalets – that kind of thing. There's a complex at the centre where they handle the straight customers. That looks to be honest enough – there's a gym an' a swimming pool, jacuzies, therapy rooms. That kind of stuff. The AID unit is built separate to that, about a quarter mile distant. Romero says he can fix me an interview with Vereker in a few days. I'll call you then.'

'OK,' Stoner said. 'I spoke to Manners.'

'What'd he say?' Antrim's voice crackled down the line. 'You get anywhere?'

'He thinks the woman was married to a guy called Eddy Scharff,' Stoner replied. 'He's checking it out.'

'Great,' said Antrim. 'I think we may be getting somewhere.'

'Yeah,' said Stoner. Wondering where.

Gerald Manners called the next day. He told Stoner that Eddy Scharff had been in Rio de Janeiro when he heard of his wife's death. He had immediately flown to Portland and arranged for the body to be returned to Dallas for burial. Manners had gathered that Scharff had spoken with the people at the Walters Institute, but was reluctant to discuss the matter any farther.

'Would it do any good bringing me in?' Stoner asked.

'No,' Manners replied. 'Eddy spoke to me because we're friends. He was pretty broken up, but he really didn't want to talk about it.'

'Did he know about your wife?' Stoner said, nervous of the delicate subject.

'I told him.' Manners's voice got flat; unemotional. 'He said he thought it must be some kind of weird coincidence.'

'Weird?' Stoner's voice was verging on anger. 'It's weird, OK. It's also more than any goddam coincidence. It has to be.'

'Eddy didn't want to hear that,' Manners said. 'He wouldn't listen. Just told me Karen was dead and he wanted to bury her with dignity. No further discussion.'

'Just like that?' Stoner grunted. 'Just like Anders.'

'Just like,' Manners agreed. 'Just like me, I guess. It could be nothing more than a natural reaction, Mike.'

'Maybe,' murmured Stoner. 'But listen, Gerry. Can you talk him round? Get something more?'

'I'll try. But I don't think I'll succeed.'

Stoner put the telephone down, wondering if he had made a big mistake turning detective. It was like living through some telefilm where the young doctor discovers horrible things going on, and before he knows it, he's neck deep in skulduggery. Trouble was, he thought, I ain't no Ben Casey. And definitely not Genevieve Bujold.

The cynical reference to *Coma* reminded him of Fay: they had seen the movie together. Afterwards, he recalled, they had eaten hotdogs and drunk beer before returning to his apartment to make love. The memory brought a sharp pang of regret to Stoner, and it took a conscious effort to push thoughts of Fay from his mind.

Antrim came through the next evening. Stoner was waiting for the call, eating a tv dinner as he vaguely realized that he had not left the apartment – except to work – for close on a week. He had been too anxious to receive Rafe's calls to risk going out.

'I saw Vereker,' Antrim announced. 'And Mike, that guy is spooky. He must be around sixty, but it's hard to tell, he's had that much plastic surgery. He looks kinda like a western Charlie Chan – yellow skin and all drawn out tight. He's a cripple. Uses this incredible wheelchair that does just about everything short of flying. He gave me the feeling he was doing the interviewing, or maybe just checking me over to see what he could improve.

'Anyway, he was helpful enough at first. Told me all about the clinic – which more or less duplicated what Romero already gave me – and told me a bit about the other side. The artificial insemination is kept understandably quiet – for the sake of the recipients – but he didn't seem to mind talking about it on the understanding it was off the record. They carry out some kind of research in the same building, but he clammed up about that. Said it was Government funded and he couldn't tell me anything without I had clearance from Washington. He also let me know I wouldn't get clearance.

'But the important thing – at least, I got that ole Antrim feeling it's important – was the way he reacted when I mentioned Karen Scharff. It's damn' near impossible to read any kind of expression on his face, but I'll swear that took him by surprise. I backed it up by mentioning the Anders woman and Lualla Manners.

'He reacted like he'd just noticed I'd tracked a dog turd into his clinical environment. Said he thought an autopsy on Karen Scharff would show she'd not complied with instructions – there was a hint the lady liked to live it up more than was good for her – and he couldn't comment on the other two. That was privileged medical information he was happy to release to the proper authorities, and no one else.

'Then he clammed up completely. Said he was needed in the research unit and called Romero in to see me off the place. I'll swear Romero was pissing his pants when he saw Vereker was upset. He made a lot of noise about how busy Vereker was and how delicate their work is, but he wanted me off and away faster than soonest.

'It's something concrete, Mike: they're scared of this getting out.'

'They'd lose a lot of money,' said Stoner. 'The whole operation could fold with that kind of publicity.'

'Maybe,' Antrim replied. 'But I got that feeling there was more than just that.'

'What you gonna do?' asked Stoner.

'Come back, I guess.' Antrim sounded reluctant. 'I'm not gonna get anything more out of Vereker or Romero, so I may as well come home and see what I can get from contacts. I'll try for a flight tonight, but I'll let you know when I get there.'

126

'OK.' Stoner paused, feeling he should add something, but not sure what. 'How's the drinking?'

'What drinking?' Antrim sounded almost smug. 'I've not touched any since I called you that first time.'

'That's good,' Stoner said. 'That's really good, Rafe.'

'Yeah.' Antrim chuckled. 'And I don't feel too bad. I'll see you, Mike.'

'Yeah.' Stoner smiled at the telephone. 'I'll see you, Rafe.'

He dropped the telephone on the cradle and fetched a Millers from the refrigerator. The beer foamed as he pulled the ringtab, and he drank from the can as he dialled Gerald Manners' apartment.

He told Manners of Antrim's report and asked the television man if he had got anywhere farther with Eddy Scharff.

'Nowhere,' Manners told him. 'Eddy buried Karen and he's gone back to Rio. I spoke to him once, but he said he'd discussed it all with the Institute and didn't want to talk about it any more. Word is, he'll be out of the country for a long time.'

'Shit!' grunted Stoner. 'Can you raise anything on Vereker?'

'I'll try,' Manners said. 'I'll let you know.'

Manners' resources were as good as he had promised. Not so good as Stoner had hoped – or maybe information on Ivan Vereker was just genuinely hard to come by – but nonetheless useful, if for no other purpose than providing a little more definition of one segment of the puzzle.

Ivan Vereker had been born in 1917 to Marta and Boris Vereker of Gdansk. There was little record of his early life – the Second World War had destroyed most sources of that information – so much of it was based on Vereker's own statements. He had studied medicine in Gdansk and Warsaw and Vienna, and during the war had enlisted in the German Army, serving in the medical corps. There was no record of his having belonged to the Nazi Party, nor any indication of his participating in anything other than strictly routine medical practice. He had applied for American citizenship in 1949, and had been accepted. The records got hazy again around this point, but if Vereker had been accepted into the United States, he had, presumably, been found clear of the Nazi taint. Or had something to offer of sufficient value that the immigration department was ready to welcome him in.

Within a remarkably short time he had become established as a successful gynaecologist. In 1962 a Texan millionaire called Charley Walters had put up the funds for the Institute named after him. Walters was dead now, but Vereker had made the Institute a resounding success. That side was easily checked. What was considerably more cloudy, was where the artificial insemination came in.

The Institute was registered with the AMA, but there was hardly any information on that aspect of its activities. Less still on the research carried out there. The funding could originate from the Pentagon, or even from the Vermont establishment of the CIA; it was not possible to find out.

Stoner ended the conversation feeling more than a little frightened. Somehow the blank patches in Vereker's life, allied with the smokescreen that seemed to hide half the Institute's activities, was threatening. It felt like something was going on, but like the man in the Dylan song, Stoner didn't know what it was. It felt like the horrors were coming out of the box in a rush now, threatening to overwhelm Stoner before he could get a clear sight of any of them, lurking around the corners of his vision like the half-seen shapes of nightmare.

He stared at the notes he had made, concentrating on the two things Manners had told him that might lead him further down whatever obscure path he had chosen to follow.

They were the titles of two papers Vereker had published. One, Stoner remembered glancing at with casual interest. It had been published in 1971, its title *The Beneficial Manipulation Of The Chromosome*. The second had appeared in 1975: *The Future In Our Genes*. At least someone, Stoner decided, had a sense of humour. He underlined the titles, making a mental note to check them out.

When he got them from the hospital library he found them almost incomprehensible. Genetics was not his speciality, but as best he could tell, the 1971 paper posited the idea of controlled insemination as a means of creating some kind of superbeing. (No Nazi connections? Stoner thought.) The second pursued the concept in greater detail, indicating to Stoner that considerable research had already been carried out.

When he asked around the hospital, he learnt that Vereker's techniques were now incorporated as standard practice in some cases. His theories had proven remarkably successful in the diagnosis – and often the treatment – of Down's Syndrome foetuses. It had also resulted in fresh thinking on prenatal care, with the end result that application of his work could now help guarantee healthy children. He was well thought of, Stoner's informant told him. It was a pity he didn't seem to be doing anything new.

Stoner was left with an impression of some kind of genius recluse, working in isolation towards the culmination of his theories.

In what, no one knew.

'How'd he get crippled?' Stoner asked, abruptly remembering that Manners had volunteered no information on that.

'There was a car smash.' The man Stoner was talking to was a short, sandy-haired gynaecologist called Wisden, who habitually tugged at his right ear lobe as he spoke. 'Happened right after the second paper was published. I heard there was spinal damage left him confined to a wheelchair.'

'Thanks.' Stoner left the man's office feeling he had gone another step down the obscure path. It was still dark, and he might still trip, but he got the feeling that a few more groping steps could bring him into the light.

And there was nothing more he could do until Rafe got back from Portland.

The telephone shrilled through the darkened apartment. Stoner woke wondering why the alarm was ringing, then realized it was still night and it wasn't the alarm, but the 'phone. He switched on the bedside spotlight and peered blearily at the clock beside the 'phone. The dimmed figures read 2.07 A.M. He lifted the 'phone.

A voice he didn't recognize said, 'Doctor Michael Stoner?'

He grunted an affirmative, rubbing at his eyes.

'This is the Dallas Police Department. Are you acquainted with a man called Rafe Antrim?'

Abruptly, Stoner wasn't sleepy any more. He swung his legs clear of the bed, an unpleasantly cold prickling sensation tracking down his spine.

'Rafe?' he answered. 'Sure. Why?'

The voice took on the formal tones of a bored policeman reading a familiar message that he knew would bring a familiar reaction.

'Rafe Antrim was found dead at the wheel of a rented car at 9.04 last night. According to the report we got from the PPD, he had been drinking heavily.'

'No!'

Stoner's interruption was automatic: pure reflex.

'Rafe had quit. He told me on the 'phone he hadn't touched booze since he landed at Portland.'

130

'An empty bottle of Old Crow was found in the wreckage,' said the voice in exactly the same tone. 'Blood samples indicated an excessive amount of alcohol in the bloodstream. The PPD is satisfied Antrim was drunk when his car went off the road.'

'No!' Stoner repeated. Then: 'Oh, Jesus Christ!'

'I'm sorry, Doctor Stoner.' It didn't sound like the man was capable of such emotion. 'But your name was found amongst the deceased's effects. He had you listed as next of kin.'

Stoner grunted, incapable of speech.

'The PPD can bury him,' continued the voice. 'Or they can ship the body down here.'

'Jesus,' Stoner said. 'I don't know.'

'Look,' said the voice, not quite showing any concern. 'You want to think about it, you let me know tomorrow. The name's Rickenbacker. Detective Colin Rickenbacker.'

'Yeah.' Stoner nodded dumbly. 'I'll call you tomorrow.'

The telephone went dead.

Stoner sat with the receiver in his hand until the electronic whining prompted him to replace the thing. After that the apartment was very silent. Stoner stood up. He needed to move about as the knowledge sank in.

Rafe was dead.

Rafe had gone to Portland to check out the Walters Institute, and now he was dead.

He had spoken to Ivan Vereker. And now he was dead.

He was dead at the wheel of a wrecked car.

With an empty bottle of Old Crow beside him and alcohol in his bloodstream.

But he had given up drinking.

And Stoner believed that.

And now he was dead.

Dead: killed. Demised. Gone. Another statistic, like Marianne Anders or Lualla Manners or Betty Ramsden or Karen Scharff. Or any of the other dead women.

131

It kept coming back to that single word: dead.

Rafe was dead.

'Oh, God,' Stoner moaned, feeling tears form. 'What have we started?'

There was no answer. The apartment was dark and empty. He stumbled against a chair, grunting as the chromed steel barked his shin, then turned on the lights.

He put them all on, as though the brilliance could drive away the dark fears coalescing in his mind. He went into the kitchen and made a pot of coffee, and for the remainder of the night he sat sipping coffee and staring into the darkness on the other side of the window.

And the single thought kept repeating in his mind: Rafe is dead.

Rafe.

Is.

Dead.

11

Fay looked up as Stoner came into the office, and felt her mouth go dry. After their last meeting she had spent a night crying into her pillow, and the next two days feeling, as her father liked to put it, lower 'n a rattlesnake's asshole. After that she had pulled herself together and got on with her life; which was, after all, hers, not Mike Stoner's. She had felt some of the confusion shared by Stoner, but in a different way. There was no doubt in her mind that there was a *proper* way to do things, and that ultimately *the authorities* could – and should – be left to handle affairs. She was, she realized, middle-class in her thinking, even bourgeois, but she couldn't help that. It was the way she was, and Mike should realize that.

She had bent the force of her considerable (albeit middle-class) will to the task of *not* thinking about Stoner. And she had succeeded, but in succeeding had walled off a part of her emotional psychology. And now Stoner was walking through the open door and the wall around her feelings was crumbling.

Her first thought was, *My God! He looks terrible*.

He did: his eyes were hollow, dark rings covering the lower lids so that the unusual pallor of his skin was emphasized. His hair was lank, untidy. The knot of his tie was tugged down from an open shirt collar that looked in need of pressing, and his face was gaunt.

Her second thought was, *What's happened to him?*

And then she knew. He looked at her with weary, reddened eyes, and his voice was hoarse as he said, 'Rafe is dead.'

The flat statement hung in the air between them and Fay didn't know if it was a barrier or a lifeline. She watched him cross the office and halt before her desk, and in that moment she knew she loved him. Maybe not enough to go on living with him; maybe not enough to marry him. But for that instant, totally.

'How?' she asked, suddenly conscious that her own voice was husky.

'He went up to Oregon,' Stoner said dully. 'To check out the Walters Institute. He called me to say he was coming back, then I got a call from the DPD. Rafe was found dead in a wrecked car. They say he'd been drinking.'

'Oh, dear God,' she whispered. 'Poor Rafe.'

'He wasn't,' Stoner said. 'He'd stopped.'

'Rafe?' She couldn't accept it, couldn't believe it. 'Rafe stopped drinking?'

'Yeah.' Stoner nodded, looking as though the motion cost him effort. 'He told me he quit the day he got there. A woman died on the 'plane. It shook him up. Enough that he quit. The last time I spoke to him, he said he hadn't touched any.'

'And you believed him?' She couldn't stop it coming out, regretting it instantly.

Fire sparkled briefly in Stoner's dull eyes. He said, 'Yeah. I believed him.'

She stared at his haggard face and knew that his belief was total; she wasn't certain she could share it. Rafe was – had been! – an alcoholic, and alcoholics were notoriously cunning. Maybe Rafe had lied to Mike. Told him he'd stopped because he wanted to reassure Mike. And then she thought, No. Rafe wouldn't lie to Mike. Not to Mike.

'So what do you think happened?'

'I don't know.' Stoner shook his head painfully. 'I sat up what was left of the night thinking about it. I didn't like what I was thinking. Fay, I think Rafe was killed.'

'Murdered?'

The single word dropped into the silence. A gunshot in the night; a faraway church bell, a single toll suddenly loud because the wind has swung around, bringing it close.

'I think it has to be.' Stoner perched on the edge of her desk, head down, hands on knees. 'He'd stopped drinking, Fay. But they found him in a car wreck with a bottle of Old Crow beside him and alcohol in his bloodstream. I think someone set it up.'

'Why?' she asked. 'Why would anyone kill Rafe?'

'He was at the Institute. He talked to Vereker.' Fay frowned, and Stoner added, 'The boss man. Rafe told me he'd mentioned the dead women. Some of them, at least. And Vereker went silent on him, and then he was shown out. The next thing, he was dead.'

'Mike,' she said, trying to impose her own logic on the situation, 'you can't know that. God! Do you realize what you're suggesting?'

'I think so.' His voice was low. She heard fear in it, and rage. Mostly, she heard determination. 'I think something is going on up there they don't want made public. I think Rafe got too close, and they killed him because they got scared he'd put something in the paper.'

'If that were so,' she fought to remain rational, 'wouldn't they – whoever *they* are – stop the paper printing?'

'Maybe they can't,' he answered, and she saw there was logic in his thinking. 'Maybe they're not quite big enough to do that. Or maybe they were afraid Rafe would tell people.'

'That means they'll be afraid of *you*.' Concern for him banished her scepticism for a while. 'Won't they link you with Rafe?'

'I guess.' Stoner nodded again. 'Rafe had me listed as next of kin.'

'God!' A cold knot of fear curdled in her soul. 'Who are they?'

'I don't know,' Stoner murmured. 'The CIA? Some other Government agency we don't even know about? If

Rafe was killed because he got too close to whatever's going on up there, then maybe they'll be looking for me.'

She touched his hand. It was hot and dry, and the fingers curled naturally into hers, entwining, seeking support. She placed both hands around his.

'What are you going to do?'

'Talk to Eddison first,' he said, a memory of his smile touching his face. 'Tell him everything I know and everything I suspect. See what he's prepared to do about it. After that? Well, there's a guy called Gerry Manners. VP of KXWTV. His wife died the same way, and he's in this thing with us. With me.'

'Eddison will tell you to leave well alone,' she said, glad that she could put the words in someone else's mouth. 'He'll tell you it's nothing to do with you.'

'Rafe is dead.' He said it slowly, emphasizing each syllable. 'That makes it something to do with me. I'm a doctor – I took an oath to preserve life, and that makes it something to do with me. I'm sorry, Fay. I'm scared as hell, but I'm in too deep to pull out now.'

Her hands tightened on his, as though the physical pressure could force her thoughts into his mind. She wanted to tell him to quit. To go to Eddison and tell him he was leaving it all. Forgetting about it. Hoping that somehow that would get back to the mysterious, terrifying *they*. But even as she thought it, she knew it was hopeless: Mike was committed now, and nothing she could say would hold him back.

Reluctantly she let go his hands and touched the intercom on her desk.

'You want me to buzz him?'

'I guess.' Stoner stood up, brushing his hair. 'Please.'

He waited while she spoke to the Assistant Administrator, then went through the door on her nod.

Eddison was back by the window, facing Stoner as the doctor came in. The light shone through his thinning reddish hair, setting a faint halo around his sharp face, leaving the features in shadow. The effect reminded Stoner of his interview with Laurence Anders.

Eddison was wearing a dark blue suit, very neat and probably from Nieman Marcus. A blue-and-red pattern hinted its way down his tie, and his wash-white shirt showed an exact half inch of cuff. He touched the knot of his tie as Stoner sat down, then settled himself in the big leather executive chair.

'Fay said you wanted to talk to me.' Eddison shrugged. 'What about?'

Stoner told him. Everything, from Marianne Anders to Rafe's death. He spoke quietly and succinctly, not allowing the emotion he felt to confuse his thoughts. He spoke of the way the women had died and the curious obscurity surrounding their deaths. He spoke of the Walters Institute and the manner of Antrim's death. He spoke of his suspicions and his fears. And while he spoke, Eddison sat silent and expressionless, his hands set flat on the surface of his desk.

When Stoner had finished, he cleared his throat.

'This is all supposition,' he said at last. 'There's not a single concrete fact to support your hypothesis.'

Stoner struggled to keep his temper.

'Fourteen have died. That we know about for sure – there may well be more. How many, I don't know, but you could find that out. Rafe Antrim is dead, and he wasn't drinking. I'm certain of that. Something is going on, and I want to know what you intend to do about it. In an official capacity.'

Eddison smiled. It was, Stoner thought, like watching a rat bare its teeth.

'Officially?' smiled the little man. 'Are you suggesting that I turn the resources of the Dallas Memorial Hospital over to some mad detective hunt? Do you really want me to spend time – which is money, Doctor – helping you nurse paranoid fantasies? For God's sake, Stoner! I can understand you're upset. I can sympathize with that, but don't ask me to join in your game.'

Stoner's hands clenched into fists. Doubt and fear and uncertainty got lost in a flood of rage that he fought hard to control. When he spoke at last it was in a voice harsh with suppressed anger.

'Does that mean you'll do nothing? Nothing at all?'

'Exactly,' said Eddison, still smiling. 'Do you honestly believe I'd risk the good name of this hospital – my own reputation – playing along with you? Good God, man! If you were a patient, I'd assign you to the psychiatric wing.'

'Rafe Antrim is dead,' Stoner repeated. 'That's a fact.'

'An alcoholic journalist drove his car off the road because he couldn't stay off the bottle.' Eddison shrugged. 'I'm sorry, but if that's what the police say, that's what I believe. You have nothing but Antrim's word to oppose that with, and the word of an alcoholic – no matter how well meaning – doesn't really count for much.'

Stoner's teeth ground together, so the next words came out almost mumbled.

'And the dead women?'

'I don't know.' Eddison flicked a scrap of lint from his lapel. 'It's not my business.'

'Life is our business,' Stoner grunted.

'For a doctor, yes.' Eddison nodded. 'But my province is the successful running of this hospital. That includes maintaining its good name. And ensuring that its doctors are the best available.'

Stoner's fist unclenched. He gripped the armrests of the chair, aware that his fingers were digging into the leather.

'Is that a threat?'

'A warning, perhaps.' With the light streaming in behind him, it was hard to tell if there was a twinkle in Eddison's eyes. 'Take it as you will, but I am concerned that your work here will suffer if you continue to pursue these wild imaginings.'

'And if I do?' Stoner asked slowly. 'If I don't give up?'

Eddison shrugged; eloquently.

'I don't see how playing detective can leave you much time for hospital work.'

Stoner felt suddenly cold. He got a flash of memory like an instant replay of a football game. He was back in the honkytonk with Rafe and Fay, and Rafe was telling him about the poisoned sheep and how the affair was hushed up with the full approval of his editor.

But now Rafe was dead.

'You're telling me I have a choice?' he said slowly. 'Forget all this, or I'm out. Right?'

'I might have put it differently,' Eddison murmured, 'but yes. That's about the size of it.'

'Fuck you!'

Stoner's temper boiled over. He came up out of the chair like an uncoiling spring and Eddison lurched back, lifting his hands as though to ward off a blow. Stoner came close to the big desk and halted with the three feet of polished teak between them. He put his hands down on the desk, leaning across it so that his face was closer to the small administrator's.

'Fuck you, Eddison. And fuck the hospital. I'll not quit.'

Eddison nodded as though approving a decision well made.

'I'll have Fay draw up the papers. I suggest you take some leave. A week, say. Think about it. If you haven't changed your mind in that time, the relevant documents will be ready.'

Stoner spun round without speaking. There wasn't much he could say, and the only thing he could think of just then was another *Fuck you*. He crossed the office and pulled the door open, closing it carefully behind him in overreaction to his desire to slam it.

Behind him, when he was sure Stoner would not return, Eddison lifted a telephone. It was a dark green 'phone, and it connected to a direct line that was not routed through the standard switchboard. Eddison began to punch a number from memory. It was an Oregon number.

'What happened?'

Fay looked at Stoner's face and got scared of the answer.

'He didn't want to know. Just like you said.' Stoner thrust his fists into the pockets of his tunic. 'He told me I was paranoid. Then he gave me a choice: I have a week to think it over. Either I give this thing up, or I get my walkin' papers.'

'Mike!' Fay's face went pale. 'That could ruin you.'

'Yeah.' Stoner nodded grimly. 'Or Eddison, if I can find out what the hell's going down.'

'You've made up your mind.' Her voice was low. Frightened.

'I don't have much choice,' Stoner said.

Fay shook her head. She wanted to cry. She wanted to kiss him. She wanted to hit him. She didn't know what she wanted.

'You do.' She sounded forlorn. 'You do, Mike.'

'Rafe is dead.' It was beginning to sound like a litany. Or a battle-cry. 'Rafe is dead, Fay.'

She nodded slowly. Then, low and tired: 'Maybe we are, too. Do you want that, Mike?'

'No.' There was sincerity in his voice. Regret, too. 'But I can't stop, Fay. Don't you see that? I can't stop because Rafe is dead.'

'Yes,' she answered. 'No. Oh, hell, Mike! I don't know.'

'I'll call you.' Stoner moved to the door. 'Tonight. OK?'

Fay nodded and Stoner went out into the corridor. He rode the elevator down and headed straight for the locker room, a curious calm settling in his mind. His choices were much simpler now; consequently, easier to make. He had no intention of giving up on his self-imposed investigation, and if that meant losing his job at the hospital – too bad. If Fay couldn't understand that, then it was merely bringing a crisis that would, sooner or later, have occurred anyway. He was committed and his conscience was clear. He changed into street clothes and went to a 'phone.

He was put straight through to Gerald Manners, who listened in silence to Stoner's report then said, 'Why not come over? Now.'

Stoner agreed and went out to the parking lot.

It was an hour before he reached the KXWTV building, leaving the Mustang in the basement carpark and taking the elevator up to the topmost level. Manners' office was everything television soaps had led him to expect of a television executive's office. The floor was thick with an oatmeal coloured carpet, the furniture all chrome and leather; there was a lot of glass about, in the furniture and the wall-to-wall windows; the solid walls were tastefully arrayed with stills, original paintings by Klee and Rauschenberg and Mondrian, and two Grammies stood in niches. Manners' desk was bigger than Eddison's or Anders', but the man came around it to shake hands with Stoner and ask him if he wanted a drink.

'It looks like there's some kind of plot,' he said. 'Now we have to decide how we're going to handle it.'

Stoner was pleasantly surprised there was no questioning of his facts. Manners accepted that Rafe had stopped drinking; that his death had to have something to do with the Walters Institute.

'A private investigator might be the answer,' Manners said, twisting his glass so that the melting ice cubes tinkled faintly against the sides. 'Someone discreet, who knows how to handle himself.'

'Maybe we should tell the police,' Stoner suggested. 'I have to speak to this guy Rickenbacker, anyway.'

Manners shook his head. 'If your theories are true, then

the fewer people in authority who know about this, the better.'

Stoner nodded, feeling the enormity of the statement sink in. It was one thing to posit conspiracy theories in the heat of anger and loss. To hear his own fears voiced calmly by this grey-haired man somehow made them real. And personally applicable – if he was right, and Rafe had been murdered, then who was next?

'Who knows so far?' Manners asked, as though sensing Stoner's thoughts.

'Fay,' Stoner replied. 'Fay Nicholas – we were living together. I told her all about it. And Eddison, at the hospital.'

'Can you trust them?'

'Fay, sure. Not Eddison.'

'A pity.' Manners freshened their drinks. 'Do you think they'll mention it to anyone?'

'Not Fay. Eddison might. Probably will if I don't go back toeing the line.'

'Forget that.' Manners smiled tightly. 'I don't want to patronize, but I can always find you work. Here, or I can put in a word; so you needn't worry.'

'Thanks.' Stoner smiled wanly. 'I appreciate that.'

'The least I could do.' Manners went over to the desk and punched the intercom. 'Pat? Can you make me an appointment with Bob Ludlow, please? As soon as possible.'

He sat down again, facing Stoner.

'I think it might be an idea if you dropped out of sight for a spell. Why don't you come out to the ranch with me?'

'OK.' Stoner was grateful for the offer: right now the thought of going home wasn't especially appealing. 'And thanks again.'

Manners shrugged: 'Maybe there's safety in numbers. Why don't you go get whatever you need now? Then meet me back here.'

'Sure,' Stoner said. 'I'll call Rickenbacker first.'

Manners gestured at the telephones on his desk. 'Do it from here. And, Mike? Don't tell him where you'll be.'

'I have to arrange for Rafe's burial.' Stoner paused with the receiver in his hand. 'He'll need to know where I am.'

'Let me look after it. If Rickenbacker needs to contact you, he can do it through this office.'

'That seems kinda callous,' Stoner protested. 'Rafe was my friend.'

'And he's dead,' said Manners coolly. 'The best service you can do Antrim is staying alive.'

'I guess,' Stoner acknowledged.

He dialled the number Rickenbacker had given him and told the detective he wanted Antrim's body flown down from Portland, all costs to be sent to Gerald Manners at KXWTV; if the detective needed to contact him, he could leave a message at the same place. While he was speaking, the intercom buzzed and Manners spoke briefly with his secretary.

'We've got an appointment with Bob Ludlow tomorrow,' he told Stoner. 'Bob's an old friend, and he runs the best PI outfit in this city. He's coming out to the ranch.'

'Good.' Stoner rubbed his unshaven jaw. 'I'll go get my stuff.'

The apartment was bright with late-afternoon sunshine as Stoner went in. Some mail had arrived, and he gathered the envelopes, setting them on one side. His coffee cup from the previous night still sat on the small table and the sheets on his bed were still rumpled. The place was empty, yet Stoner got that near-intangible feeling of another presence. As though someone had entered the apartment in his absence and left behind some lingering memory of their presence. He glanced around the rooms, seeing nothing obviously disturbed. He sniffed the air, wondering if he had subconsciously registered a smell: a cigarette,

143

maybe, or after-shave. There was nothing. He checked his papers, but could see no sign of disturbance, and when he tried to recall the exact placement of things, he found it impossible. He was getting paranoid again, he told himself. This was pure imagining, and maybe Eddison was right – he was ready for the psychiatric wing.

But the feeling remained as he tossed clothes into a bag and gathered up his shaving things.

He zippered the bag and set it down by the door. He had said he would call Fay, and he wanted to get the call made. Wanted to tell her what he was doing and try to make her understand it. After that, she could decide. He checked his watch, then dialled the number of Fay's apartment.

'Fay?'

'Mike! Are you all right?'

'I'm OK. I'm in the apartment. Listen, Fay. I'm staying over with Gerry Manners – the guy I mentioned? We figure that if I'm right about this thing, it's safer. Don't tell anyone where I am, OK?'

There was a pause, then a sigh.

'Do you know what you're doing, Mike?'

'Yes. Can I see you?'

Another pause, longer. Then: 'I don't think that's a good idea right now, Mike. I'm sorry, but I think this business with Rafe has gotten to you more than you know.'

'I'm not crazy, Fay. I have to find out to satisfy myself. I owe Rafe that much.'

'Rafe is dead, Mike. You're still alive. You've got a career to think about.'

'This is more important, Fay.'

'Than your career? Than us?'

'No. Maybe. Hell, I don't know.'

Another sigh.

'I think that says it, Mike. You don't know.'

'About us? I do, Fay. I know I want you. But you have to meet me halfway.'

'I have to play *The Hardy Boys*, too, Mike? No: I don't.

You talk about us meeting halfway, but can you see my side?'

'I can see you're worried, honey. I know you're thinking about my career. But I have to do this.'

'You don't, Mike. You don't have to do it. You're not the hero of some damn' Western. Rafe died and that's sad. But you have a future, Mike. And you're destroying it.'

'If that's how you see it, then there's not much point talking.'

Stoner's hand tightened on the receiver as he waited for her to reply.

'No. I don't suppose there is. Call me if you come to your senses.'

The telephone went dead. Stoner set it back on the rests and sat there staring at the silent shape. So that was it. That was how the affair ended. Not the way he'd thought; definitely not the way Fay had expected. No great drama, not even tears. Just a few terse sentences spoken into a cup of plastic: it's over, so goodbye. Hell! he thought. Maybe it's best. I'm how I am and Fay is how she is. Maybe it was a mistake from the start. Maybe we'd never have worked out, not in the long run. Maybe I'm better off without her.

But alongside those thoughts, like the counterface of a penny, there were the others: You don't want it to be over. Maybe you can work it out. Maybe you should call her back.

Stoner sniffed noisily and picked up his bag. A few minutes later he was behind the wheel of the Mustang, heading back to the KXW building.

Manners' ranch could have been used as a set for *Dallas*. The house itself sprawled at the centre of a vast, carefully-tended lawn patterned with flowerbeds, protected from the wasting Texas sun by a system of sprinklers. The building was stone and stucco, a balcony with what felt like about a mile of wrought iron work running around the upper level. The first floor was largely glass, great sliding doors opening onto large, airy rooms, a sun deck extension of the balcony shading a patio that ran out to the Olympic-size swimming pool. A quarter mile distant there were plain wood buildings and corrals with prime-stock Herefords, and way off a line of dippers nodded against the heat haze.

Manners steered his Ferrari into a giant garage, and Stoner parked the Mustang between the sleek, scarlet car and a Stingray. He wondered if the Stingray had belonged to Lualla Manners.

His room lived up to the exterior expectations of the house. It was nearly as big as Stoner's apartment, the door opening onto a living area, with the bedroom and a king-size bathroom beyond. A big colour tv with VCR attached dominated the living area. A row of shelves beside the tv held video tapes; there was a selection of liquor in a mirror-fronted cabinet; and the room contained a small library, the books ranging from Stephen King to Arthur Koestler. Stoner unpacked his bag with a slightly unreal feeling. Living like James Bond, he thought. Only Bond always knew what he was doing. And he had a lot more help.

He shaved and changed into fresh clothes, then joined Manners on the patio.

Off to the west, the sun was getting close to the edge of the world. Mellow light flooded the ranch house, gleaming brilliant off the glass. The pool looked cool and blue and very inviting, and there was an appetizing smell coming from the kitchen. Manners put a martini in his hand.

'Nice place,' Stoner murmured, recognizing the under-statement.

'I like it.' Manners lounged in a big wicker chair, shirt-sleeved now. 'It's big for me without Lu, but I don't want to give it up.'

146

'No,' Stoner murmured. 'Some things you don't want to give up.'

'Problems?' Manners sensed the pain in Stoner's reply. 'Fay?'

Stoner nodded.

'Anything I can do?' Manners plucked the olive from his glass.

'No.' Stoner shook his head. 'Nothing anyone can do. When do we meet Ludlow?'

'He's coming by eleven o'clock.'

'Good,' Stoner said, feeling a need for action. For something to take his mind off his doubts.

12

Robert Ludlow was a stocky, semi-bald man who might have passed for anything but a private investigator. Stoner was not sure just how a private investigator was supposed to look, but the avuncular detective in the crumpled brown suit was not his idea. At least, not until the introductions had been made and Ludlow settled down to business. Then he became suddenly different: sharper, somehow, his questions cutting direct to the heart of things.

He absorbed Stoner's story in silence, brown eyes fixed unwinkingly on the doctor's face.

When Stoner was finished he said, 'Eddison could be right, you know. Maybe it is all coincidence.'

'No.' Stoner shook his head. 'I'm certain it's not.'

'You got reason,' grunted Ludlow. 'That's for sure.'

'You'll handle it?' Manners asked. 'You can name the fee.'

Ludlow fetched an ugly-looking cheroot from inside his coat, concentrating on getting the thing lit before he replied.

'The fee'll be standard, Gerry. You know that. Question is, do you realize what you're asking me to do?'

He sat back in the wicker chair, blowing clouds of evil-smelling smoke into the warm morning air, his eyes studying the Japanese gardener working methodically through the flower beds.

'You believe these women are dying because of the artificial insemination techniques used at this Institute. You think about that. Think about the reputation you say this place has.'

Manners and Stoner watched him, waiting for him to continue. On the table, the coffee pot bubbled quietly.

'They're as good as folks say,' Ludlow continued, 'it can't be the technique, can it? Hell, AID's not new, and this place sounds like it has it off to a fine art. So you got to look for some other reason.' He turned to Stoner. 'You're the doc here, Mike. You tell us what else to look for.'

Stoner sipped coffee, realizing he hadn't thought it through that far. He had been limited by his sense of horror, concerned only with the dead – and dying? – women and the conviction that the Walters Institute was somehow responsible.

Then he gasped and said, 'Jesus! The only other thing it could be is the sperm itself.'

Ludlow puffed more smoke. Manners set his cup down and leant forwards in his chair.

'It has to be the sperm!' Stoner said, excited. 'Like Bob says, the techniques must be OK. We know the women were healthy – plus, an incompatibility ratio like this is way too high. And it goes too far for normal foetal incompatibility. It has to be the sperm.'

'OK.' Ludlow studied the tip of his cheroot. 'See where that leaves us? The next logical step is to locate the donor. And I don't suppose the people up at the Walters Institute are gonna hand me a list of names. That kind of stuff will be classified – locked away in a file up there. Or maybe the name is only on computer. Even if we can get a name, what then? What's it prove?'

'It has to prove something,' Stoner said. 'Why else would they kill Rafe?'

'That's not the point,' Ludlow answered. 'We can assume something's going on. We can assume somebody doesn't want it made public. We can assume the donated sperm is responsible. But how do we find out why? Even if I get a name – and let's assume that all the women got the same sperm, because if we don't we got a real rats' nest – then what? You gonna go to the guy and say, "Hey, feller, we think your sperm's killing ladies. How's about giving

149

us a sample?" That's the only way you're gonna know, isn't it?'

'I guess,' Stoner admitted. 'Yeah.'

'So we got problems,' Ludlow grunted. 'You see?'

'Sure.' Manners cut in, coolly authoritative. 'But it's a step farther on. Right? And just now I don't see any other step we can take.'

'No,' agreed the detective. 'You got me there.'

'Have we?' asked Manners. 'Will you take it?'

Ludlow looked at his cheroot some more. As though deciding he didn't like it after all, he ground it out.

'If Antrim was killed, then I could be up against something big.' A slow smile spread across his pleasantly ugly face. 'That's gonna cost you extra.'

'Thanks,' Manners said, smiling. 'Thanks a lot, Bob.'

'Hell!' Ludlow shrugged. 'I was fond of Lu, Gerry. Fond of you, too. I'll do what I can.'

'How?' Stoner asked. 'Or is that classified?'

'I'll take a vacation.' Ludlow patted his bulky stomach. 'I could use to lose a bit of weight, so I'll book in as a straight guest. Take a slimming cure on Gerry's expenses. While I'm up there . . . Well, I always did have a healthy sense of curiosity.'

'It could be dangerous,' warned Manners. 'Don't forget Antrim.'

'I'm not.' The smile left Ludlow's face, and for a moment it looked hard and calculating. 'I'll tread real cautious.'

He stood up and shook hands, then walked, vaguely bear-like, to his dusty Lincoln. The engine growled into life and he waved through the windshield as he swung the car around and steered down the long tarmacadamed road to the gate.

'He's good,' Manners said reassuringly. 'The best.'

'I hope so,' Stoner replied. 'I hope so.'

* * *

150

Ludlow drove back to his office on Westmoreland. For the first time in longer than he cared to remember, he felt genuine excitement about a case. He enjoyed the sense of mystery shrouding this thing – the idea of not knowing exactly what he was looking for, or where it would lead. His fondness for Gerry Manners, and his memories of Lualla, had a deal to do with it, but mostly it was the keen sense of anticipation that was pumping adrenalin through his veins the way it hadn't pumped in too long. He docked his car in the subterranean park and took the elevator up to his suite on the sixth floor. He told his secretary to get him a booking at the Walters Institute, using his real name, but – should they enquire – telling them he was an insurance broker. He felt he had handled enough insurance cases to talk up a decent cover, should it prove necessary.

One hour later he had his booking and his flight out of Dallas confirmed. He was scheduled to attend the Walters Institute for a two-week reduction therapy course in seven days. He told his secretary to keep it quiet and then set in motion a process of information gathering designed to glean him as much information on the Institute, Ivan Vereker, and Rafe Antrim as was available.

In three days he had it. And it wasn't much.

Not so much as he had hoped for, nor so much as he had expected.

The stuff on Rafe Antrim was pretty standard and Ludlow compiled a dossier that told most of the newspaperman's life story. It didn't shed much light on the mystery, though it made the detective wonder if Antrim hadn't been lying when he told Stoner he had quit drinking. The man had a lousy record of alcoholism. But Stoner had shown complete confidence in his friend's assurances, and Ludlow felt confident enough of the doctor's sincerity to go along with him. At least until concrete proof contradicted him.

What really convinced him, however, was the absence

of information on the less public aspects of the Institute, and on Ivan Vereker. His sources were the best available to a private citizen and, given the Freedom of Information Act, should have produced more. To Ludlow's experienced eye, the vagueness of the material spread across his desk indicated some kind of cover-up. To a casual reader, the documents he had amassed might have seemed perfectly normal, but to Ludlow there were too many grey areas. Too many incidences of *No Known Details* or *Information Not Available*.

The more he studied his notes, the more eager he became to get to work.

While Ludlow was busy preparing his ground, Stoner was bored.

Manners left for the television station each day around 8.00 A.M., and until he returned, Stoner was mostly alone. The novelty of the luxurious house rapidly wore off, and he found himself looking for company. The ranch was a working outfit, and the hands were too busy to spend much time jawing with one of the boss's guests. The servants were Mexican and discreet: Stoner was a guest, and guests did not mingle with the staff. He swam each morning, and took to riding, but more and more, he found himself missing work. And missing Fay.

Around the end of the second week – five days after Ludlow had called to say he was flying out that afternoon – Stoner gave in to temptation and dialled the hospital. He spoke to Jenny, who told him Fay had requested an unpaid vacation, and had left Dallas three days ago. So far as Jenny knew, she had gone to see her folks in Houston, and no, she hadn't left any message, but if Mike was feeling lonely . . .

Why not? Stoner thought. And made a date for that evening.

He arranged to pick Jenny up at her apartment, then

decided to stop off at his own place to check his mail before meeting her. He left word with the servants before climbing into the Mustang for the drive into town.

It was dusk as he left, and the link road connecting to US 75 was dark. Stoner flicked on his lights, holding the automobile to a steady fifty-five in obedience to regulations. Apart from a pick-up that turned into the ranch, the road was empty. The air was showing the first chill, and he wound up his windows, enjoying the sensation of movement through the growing night.

He turned onto 75 and headed south, towards the lights of the city. His speed climbed to sixty, and he kept his eyes on the road ahead, wary for radar traps. This far out, the highway was sparsely populated with vehicles. There was no reason he should have singled out the nondescript late model Chevy that pulled into the fast lane behind him as he passed the Princeton interchange.

He was aware of the lights shining in his rear-view mirror, and pulled over to clear the lane. The Chevy came up fast, drawing alongside the Mustang, and Stoner waited for it to go by. It did not. Instead, it ran level before swerving abruptly to the right.

Stoner cursed, hauling his wheel over as the sedan cut across his nose. Brake lights glowed an angry red on the Chevy's tail and Stoner hit his own pedal, feeling the Mustang's tail shudder slightly as the four discs bit. Mildly irritated, he muttered something about crazy drivers and swung back into the overtaking lane, accelerating to pass the Chevy.

The sedan speeded up and Stoner glanced sideways, expecting to see a kid grinning at him in challenge of a race. Instead, he saw a thickset man with short-cropped hair and a broken nose, wearing a grey jacket. On the passenger seat there was a thin-faced man with tidy hair and a dark suit. He was looking across at Stoner and he was grinning. He went on grinning as the Chevy moved inexorably sideways, crowding the Mustang so that Stoner hit the brakes again. This time the Chevy did not speed up. The thickset man glanced to the side and adjusted his own speed, still easing his wheel over.

The nose of the sedan caught Stoner's forward wing. There was a rasping crash and the Mustang shuddered, bouncing across the road. Stoner shouted, fighting the wheel as the automobile threatened to go into a skid. There was a second *thud*! and the nose of the Mustang was forced over the fast lane. The nearside front wheel hit the kerb of the safety barrier and mounted the elevation. Stoner stamped hard on the brakes, seeing sparks fly as the Mustang's nose was forced against the metal dividing rail. His speed dropped to thirty and the Chevy surged ahead again. Stoner sounded his horn, then lifted his own speed as anger replaced the rush of fear. The Chevy slowed, letting Stoner draw up alongside.

'What the hell are you trying?' he bellowed. 'You crazy?'

If the Chevy's driver heard him through the windows, he gave no sign. Just grinned like a wooden Indian and hauled his wheel over again.

Stoner couldn't quite believe it as he saw the Chevy swing towards him a fourth time.

The fender of the sedan hit the Mustang's wheel, threatening to spin Stoner around into the crash barrier. He accelerated, then felt the fender snag on the rim of the wheel arch. The sedan was still crowding him to the right as he tapped the brake pedal, gaining sufficient leeway to ease over and tug the arch free. The Chevy swung away, then back. Stoner put the gas pedal on the floor, shifting down into third so that the Mustang's engine roared, the car surging eagerly ahead. He jumped the gear stick up into fourth, wincing as the dinning of another blow rang through the interior and the tail veered sharply to the right. He kept his foot down, pulling clear of the sedan as he fed power to the three-and-a-half litre motor. The hell with speed traps, he decided. If a patrolman wanted to pull him in for speeding, he was more than welcome.

The rev counter swung into the yellow and he pushed the shift into fifth, sending the speedometer needle past the eighty mark.

The Chevy accelerated faster than any standard production line saloon had a right to. Stoner was topping eighty, but the other car was closing fast. He glanced in his mirror, seeing the lights coming up behind him, and pushed the Mustang to ninety. Ninety-five. A straight hundred. And the Chevy was still closing. Closing fast enough that the headlights were blinding in his mirror and the nose of the sedan was touching the tail of the Mustang.

Stoner felt the impact shove him forwards against his safety belt. He was doing one hundred and ten now, concentrating on the road and the scattering of vehicles ahead. The Chevy nudged him again, then a third time, each blow lurching the Mustang so that the wheel threatened to jump free of Stoner's grip. He felt very cold now, and there was sweat on his face, cool and sticky on his back. The two men in the car weren't kids looking for fun. Nor were they rednecks working out some kind of redneck grudge. From the brief glimpse he had gotten of them, they looked tough and self-possessed. Like professionals.

Like Mafia hitmen.

Or CIA operatives.

Stoner's sweat got colder and a raw ache in the pit of his stomach identified itself as naked fear.

Another shock vibrated through the Mustang, and he felt the sports car shudder and begin to fishtail. He corrected the impending skid and tried to draw away from the sedan.

The Chevy pulled back, then accelerated again, coming up alongside. From the corner of his eye, Stoner could see the driver, face impassive, glancing sideways as he calculated his angle. Then the Chevy was moving over again and Stoner swung his wheel, scorching across three lanes. He pulled slightly ahead of the Chevy, gaining a little distance as the saloon followed him over the highway. It began to gain, and Stoner felt panic as he realized the driver was lining up to crowd him into the barrier. The traffic was getting thicker as they came closer to the city, and Stoner realized that if they continued at their current speeds, one of them – most likely him – was going to pile into some innocent traveller.

The Chevy came level again, swerving abruptly to smash its full length against the Mustang. There was a terrific clatter, then an ugly scraping sound as the thickset man paced Stoner with the heavy saloon leaning its weight against the lighter car. Stoner felt the Mustang begin to shift across the road and turned his own wheel, fighting to stay clear of the barrier. He boosted his speed, then as suddenly hit the brakes. Metal ripped from the Mustang's side as the Chevy surged ahead, but the pressure was gone for a moment. Stoner jammed the brake pedal against the floor, fighting the swing of the tail as the Chevy began to drop back. He pushed the shift into fourth and fed gas to the engine, feeling the Mustang surge forwards to overtake the Chevy. Up ahead he saw a turn-off sign, the directional arrow gleaming bright and promising in his headlights. He shifted back into fifth, holding the gas pedal on the floor in a desperate attempt to stay ahead of the Chevy long enough to reach the intersection.

The saloon moved up beside him and then veered away. For an instant Stoner thought they had given up, but then he saw the driver was merely looking to gain extra momentum as he swung his wheel over and closed again on Stoner's vehicle.

The turn-off was close now, and getting closer with each terrifying moment.

And then Stoner was on it. He yanked his wheel over and took the turn in a wild skid. He felt the tail swing round, slamming against the barrier so that a cascade of sparks marked his exit point, and then he was fighting to bring the big automobile back under control as two wheels lifted clear of the road and the Mustang threatened to spill over.

It came down with a teeth-jarring thud and Stoner snatched the shift down as he braked and swung wild around the descending curves. A Cadillac let loose a klaxon blast as he veered around it, almost forcing the big car off the road, but then he was down onto the Lyndon B. Johnson Freeway and when he chanced a look in his mirror, there was no sign of the Chevy.

He took the first turn-off and pulled to the side of the road. He was breathing heavily, and as delayed shock set in, he began to shake.

The men in the Chevy had tried to kill him. They had tried to force him off the road. Maybe that was how they'd killed Rafe. The cold certainty that his life was in danger transformed the knot of fear in his belly to a curdling assurance of sickness. Abruptly, Stoner yanked his safety belt clear of the socket and climbed out of the Mustang. He stumbled to the kerb and doubled over, spitting thin bile onto the indifferent concrete. When he was finished, he wiped his mouth and surveyed the damage to his car. The nearside forward wing was crumpled and there was a deep dent in the driver's door. Long scratch marks ran down the side of the car, naked metal showing through the black paint. One tail light was shattered, and the rear fender was a dented mess. The tyre that had hit the kerb looked in danger of rupture. Stoner climbed back inside and drove slowly to his apartment.

The place was dark and Stoner flicked on the lights with an unpleasant sense of anticipation. There was only anticlimax: the apartment had that dead feeling of a place left empty for a spell. There were some letters waiting for him, and amongst them he recognized the franking mark of the hospital. He picked that one up and tore it open. It was Eddison's promise fulfilled: the services of Doctor Michael Cauldwell Stoner were no longer required by Dallas Memorial. His employment documents were enclosed together with a severance cheque. Stoner folded the stuff into his pocket. It didn't seem very important just now.

The sound of the telephone startled him. He lifted the receiver and got another shock.

A voice with hard New England vowel sounds said, 'You were lucky back there, Stoner. You only get one chance. Next time you're dead.'

The sound of the receiver going down punctuated the sentence. Stoner swallowed hard, feeling sweat start afresh across his forehead, down his back. He set the 'phone down and sucked in air. Let it out slow. He felt frightened. He wished he wasn't involved; wished there had been some other doctor around when the call about Marianne Anders came in.

But he was involved. And Rafe was dead. And there was nothing to do but go ahead. And hope.

He poured himself a big measure of Jack Daniels and drank it neat. Then he took a shower and changed into a clean shirt. After that, he left the Mustang parked and took a cab to Jenny's apartment.

She took his mind off his problems, and by the early hours of the morning he was concentrating whole-heartedly on something else.

13

The heatwave that had gripped the Eastern Seaboard was loosening its hold. In Boston there was already a hint of winter in the air. Not yet enough to bring the fur coats into regular use, but sufficiently chilly in the evenings to justify some small display.

Joe Alexander took sour pleasure from his ability to identify a good fur at first glance. Thirty years as a doorman, working his way upwards from the medium-price hotels to the luxury establishments and then into the classy apartment blocks where the work was easier, had given Joe a nodding acquaintance with the rich. Mrs Abregard in 14C wore wild mink from Ralph Lauren – that was class. The new woman in number 6 wore a fox from Christie Brothers – not so good, but not bad. Last year, Mrs Gilford had worn Russian sable from Ben Kahn – which was pretty good (Joe had a fondness for sable). And the single girl in 19A had a broadtail lamb from Swakara – Joe wasn't sure about that yet.

What he was sure about, was that he didn't recognize the fur on the woman sitting in the Maserati down in the sub-basement parking area. Come to that, he didn't recognize the woman, either. Which was odd, as the car belonged to the Halyards, and Joe prided himself on knowing all his tenants. Tom Halyard was out of town for a couple of weeks, so maybe Mrs Halyard had loaned the car to a friend.

If that was the case, the friend was about to receive the full weight of Joe's wrath. It was the superintendent's night off, and Joe was feeling pissed off at being called away from his normal duties because some brainless rich bitch (who was most likely drunk out of her skull, or high on something) was sitting in the Maserati blocking off three parking spaces.

Joe went up to the car wondering who the hell it was sitting behind the wheel. Then he recognized Laura Halyard and began to wonder if she was sick. Her face was unusually pale, her eyes staring straight ahead; trance-like. Her mouth was open, and as Joe got close to the window he saw that her fur was discoloured with vomit. Which was no way to treat a Bill Blass lynx.

Joe opened the door and started to say, 'You all right, Mrs Halyard?' But the sentence never got finished, be-cause Joe found himself looking in at a corpse.

Laura Halyard was slumped in the wrap-around seat with blood all over the lower part of her coat. The fur was matted with it. It was thick and stinking over her legs, pooling on the seat beneath her, soaked through her silk evening gown. Joe hadn't seen that much blood since a shell from a King Tiger had landed in the hut on the outskirts of Bastogne, and blown the dogfoot beside him clean in two. He gagged, realizing he was about to vomit, and staggered away. He had vomit down the front of his shirt as he dialled the BDP and gasped a near-hysterical request for a police car and an ambulance.

In Great Falls, Montana, the weather was already cold. There had been a couple of snow flurries – not much, but enough to get folks thinking winterwise.

Jean Dupré was bundled up in a Halston ski jacket with a silk sweater from Anne Klein underneath. Her pants were a thick-wool knit from Ferragamo, tucked inside insulated après-ski boots bought on her last trip to Aspen. She was still cold, though, and the idea of.taking a solitary hike was rapidly souring. The chilly air was doing nothing except exacerbate her headache, and the pain in her belly was getting worse. She decided to turn back for home and see what a hot toddy with plenty of rum in it would do.

And maybe just one more of the capsules – one extra wouldn't hurt.

It was three days before the search parties found the body. By then animals had been at it, and consequently it was very difficult to ascertain the exact cause of death.

In Kansas City, Missouri, a team of doctors and nurses laboured most of one night to save the woman brought in by her hysterical husband. They were unsuccessful: the bleeding wouldn't stop, and they couldn't pump enough new blood into her to save her life.

After they had shut down the life support machinery and cleaned up, one of the nurses glanced at the clothing forgotten in a corner of the emergency room.

'Pity it's all spoiled,' she remarked. 'You see the labels?'

Her companion shook her head.

'Nice,' said the first nurse. 'I always wanted an Armani outfit. And did you see the shoes? Gucci! Pity they're all bloody.'

Two miles off the Miami coast a Naval cutter answered a distress call. The medic on board the Navy vessel was neither trained nor equipped to handle the emergency. When he got on board the yacht he shook his head and swore as he saw the screaming woman with blood spurting from between her legs. He did what little he could, but the haemorrhaging woman died a quarter mile out from St Francis Hospital.

Amongst the emergency services standing by were the police. When they went on board the yacht, they found a full kilo of cocaine. The woman's husband was arrested. Offering the MPD men five hundred dollars apiece didn't help his case.

* * *

In New York a performance of *Aïda* at the Metropolitan was brought to a halt when a woman in one of the boxes began to scream louder than the performers. She was rushed to hospital, but was found dead on arrival.

Both the box at the Metropolitan and the ambulance required extensive cleaning to remove the blood and the fetid smell.

In Chattanooga, a dinner party was interrupted when Denise Chatham complained of sudden nausea. She assured her hosts it was nothing to do with the food or the excellent wine – just one of those dreadfully annoying things that pregnant women must suffer. They bade her and her husband goodnight, promising to renew the date as early as was convenient. And Denise would look after herself, wouldn't she?

They never saw Denise Chatham again, because she died on the way home. They never saw Clyde again, either. Clyde Chatham panicked when his wife began to scream, moaning that something was eating her up from inside. Clyde took his Ferrari up to one hundred and fifteen in his rush to get Denise to a hospital, and when she clutched at his arm in the final throes of her agony, he went off the road between Riverside and Wilder.

Both bodies were burned in the ensuing explosion.

On a New Mexico back road five miles out from Mosquero a Highway Patrolman called Vincent Klinger approached a Camaro with its nose on the sand and its tail skewed across the road.

The car was empty, and Klinger suspected foul play because there was blood on the drive seat and the inside of the automobile smelled, as he put it later, 'kinda weird'. He cocked the Combat Magnum he was holding in his right hand and set to following the trail of blood spots leading off into the desert. The farther he went, the thicker the trail got, no longer spots, but a definite line, drawing flies in the late afternoon sunshine. He was feeling distinctly nervous when he saw the huddled shape resting in a hollow surrounded by cholla, and circled around a few times before approaching.

When he turned the woman onto her back he took one look at the mess coming from between her legs and set off at a run for his Harley Davidson. The ambulance crew that finally arrived gave Klinger a sedative before they carried the plastic bodybag away.

'It was like she'd crawled into that goddam hollow to die,' Klinger told them back at headquarters. 'Like a hurt animal. No one should die like that.'

In Atlanta, Albuquerque, San Antonio, Macon; in St Paul and San Diego, Charleston and Sacramento; in Washington and Houston and Cheyenne and Omaha, women died.

Two collapsed in Paris, France. One in London, England. Three in Zurich. Four in the Bahamas.

There were more, but each one was an individual death, and the few doctors who took time out to wonder at the cause were occupied enough with other matters to forget their initial curiosity.

Had anyone pursued the matter, collated facts, they would have seen a pattern. All of the dead women shared certain characteristics.

They were all aged between twenty-seven and thirty-two.

They were all healthy, in peak condition.

They were all of above average intelligence; in three cases, with IQ levels approaching the two hundred mark.

They were all wealthy.

They were all pregnant.

But married to sterile men.

They had all attended the Walters Institute.

No one collated these facts. No one thought to – after all, one dead woman, no matter how curious the manner of her death, hardly represented an epidemic.

No one, that was, except the three men already involved. And they had no direct access to the sources that would have revealed the rising level of fatalities. Perhaps if they had, they might have been able to raise some kind of alarm, even force *the authorities* to mount an investigation. But Robert Ludlow was in Oregon, losing several pounds and thinking about breaking into the inner sanctums of the Institute, and Stoner and Manners were running scared.

Very scared indeed now.

14

Stoner took a cab back to the ranch, arriving as Manners was eating breakfast. The television executive looked relieved to see him, and curious that he wasn't driving the Mustang. When Stoner explained why, the grey-haired man frowned; it was difficult to tell if he was angry or frightened.

'That proves it,' he murmured. 'There has to be some kind of conspiracy.'

'It proves we'd better be careful.' Stoner helped himself to coffee. 'You think we should tell the police now?'

'No.' Manners shook his head. 'What can you prove? A couple of crazies tried to run you off the road? That happens every day. Best thing is to stay close to home. I'll have a guard put on the gate and some of the boys stick around here. You're not planning any more romantic adventures, are you?'

Stoner shook his head ruefully, not sure the night with Jenny had been worth that kind of risk.

'Maybe I should call Fay,' he said. 'She could be in danger.'

'Do that.' Manners rose decisively to his feet. 'I'll organize a guard.'

Stoner picked up the patio 'phone and dialled Houston. His call was answered by Fay's mother, sounding surprised – and pleased – to hear from him.

'Mike? It's good to speak with you. How are you?'

'I'm fine, Margaret.' He guessed that Fay hadn't told her parents of the separation; or that Margaret Nicholas was being tactful. 'Is Fay there?'

'Here?' There was surprise in her voice. 'No, Mike. Isn't she with you?'

165

Stoner got the kind of feeling that normally comes only in a dream: when the dreamer is walking along a perfectly ordinary path, suddenly to put a foot down and find there's nothing underneath. Just a big, dark pit. And he starts to fall.

'Mike? Are you there, Mike?'

Margaret Nicholas's voice cut into his fear.

'Huh? Yeah. Yeah, I'm here, Margaret. You say Fay's not there?'

'No. No, Mike, she's not. Is everything all right?'

'I don't know.' Stoner wasn't sure what to say. 'I thought she'd come down on a visit.'

'To us?' Now the woman sounded confused, anxiety echoing in her placid voice. 'Has something happened, Mike?'

'We had an argument,' he said, not wanting to involve her. 'Fay took some vacation time. She left Dallas four days ago. She left a message she was visiting with you.'

'Well, she's not here,' said Margaret. 'We've not heard from her since two weeks ago.'

'Maybe I got it mixed up.' Stoner didn't believe himself. 'I'll call the apartment.'

Before Fay's mother could ask him anything more, Stoner rang off. The fear he had felt as the two men in the Chevy tried to run him off the road returned, cold and ugly. He dialled the number of Fay's apartment and listened to the buzz, counting seconds as he prayed for an answer. He reached twenty-seven before he gave up and called Dallas Memorial. He asked for Eddison.

'Stoner?' The Assistant Administrator's voice was unctuous with self-satisfaction. 'It's too late to reconsider.'

'I'm not,' Stoner snapped. 'Where's Fay?'

'Miss Nicholas?' Was Eddison's tone wary? Or was that paranoia? 'She took some vacation time.'

'She's not there?' Stoner's grip tightened on the telephone. 'Where is she, Eddison?'

'Visiting her parents in Houston, I believe.' Eddison was cool now. 'And I have work to do . . .'

Stoner put the receiver down. His mouth felt dry, and he shivered in the warm morning sunshine. There was a voice inside his head telling him Fay had changed her mind. It was nothing more dramatic than that. She had decided to go off someplace alone, or maybe with friends. That was it – nothing to get panicky about.

He knew the voice was lying. It was all too coincidental. First Rafe, then the attempt on his life, now Fay was missing. He looked around the patio: it seemed horribly normal. Manners' breakfast plate, a half-eaten slice of bacon smeared with congealing egg, sat beside a folded newspaper. Coffee bubbled in the pot, two empty cups beside it. A Mexican came softly from the house and began to clear the things away. A woman was singing in the kitchen, her voice tuneful, half-heard. Stoner recognized some of the words: *Adiós, mi corazón.* The sun was shining out of a clear blue sky, and high up three buzzards were spinning circles on the thermals.

Stoner realized that his hands were clenched into fists. He forced them to relax as he took a deep breath and let it out slow. Then he took off at a run after Manners.

'Gerry!' The grey-haired man turned from the entrance to the barn, crease lines showing on his forehead as he heard the urgency in Stoner's voice. 'They've got Fay, Gerry!'

'You're sure?' Manners peered anxiously at Stoner's face. 'You've checked?'

'She's not with her folks. She's not at home. She left the hospital four days ago. They must have her.'

'Slow down.' Manners rubbed one fresh-shaved cheek. 'You can't be certain. Maybe she stayed here.'

'There's no answer from her place.' Stoner's voice was harsh. 'For Chrissakes, Gerry! They've got her.'

Manners nodded, thoughtfully rather than in agreement. His pale eyes got hooded, then he looked back at

167

Stoner with the firm air of decision that the doctor had noticed on their first meeting.

'She could be out, Mike. Look, don't go searching for her. Whatever you do, stay close to the house. Keep trying her number – if you don't get an answer by tonight, we'll talk it over.'

He put a hand on Stoner's elbow and began to walk him back to the house. His calm was reassuring. Not much, but enough that the immediate panic wore off and Stoner listened as he gave careful instructions.

'From now on, we take care. There'll be a couple of hands watching you all the time from now on. And neither of us goes out alone. There's nothing we can do until we hear from Bob Ludlow, so we sit tight and base our next move on his findings. That's all we can do, Mike – just sit tight.'

Stoner nodded, hating the logic that condemned him to inaction. It was as though he stood at the centre of a darkened room, the only illuminated object, and in the shadows around him forces moved. Malign forces, threatening him. Threatening Fay. He slumped in a chair, watching as Manners and a heavily-built cowboy climbed into the Ferrari and the sleek scarlet automobile snarled into life. A pick-up moved away from the barn, heading for the gate in the wake of the Ferrari. Stoner noticed that the cowboy in the passenger seat was holding two Winchester carbines. He saw two more hands walking long-legged towards the patio, and guessed they were his bodyguards. They were dressed in faded levis and denim workshirts. They looked tough, well-able to handle themselves in a honky-tonk brawl. Stoner wondered how they'd handle themselves against the trained operatives of whatever organization he had crossed, and was glad to see that the taller of the two men was wearing a gunbelt with a massive Ruger Blackhawk holstered on the right hip, and the other had a Winchester pump cradled under his arm.

They introduced themselves as Bo and Luke, telling Stoner to ignore them.

That was difficult. Their presence was a constant reminder of the hornets' nest he had stirred up, that he was no longer free to come and go as he pleased. And a prison – no matter how luxurious – remains a place of confinement. He took a swim, noticing as he went into the house to change that Bo climbed lazily to his feet and began to patrol the building. When he emerged again, the cowboy sauntered back to the patio and folded his rangy body into a chair. The Winchester pump lay on the table, close to him.

Stoner talked to them some, and they played cards, but mostly he spent the day in a fury of anticipation, eager for Manners' return.

When the television executive got back they drank martinis inside the house: suddenly it seemed unwise to chance the darkening patio. They ran the problem through until they were rehashing second-hand arguments and found themselves forced to admit that their only course of action was to do nothing. Stoner had tried Fay's number at thirty minute intervals throughout the day. Manners had called Ludlow's organization and had them check the airport, bus stations, and the AmTrak depot. A Fay Nicholas had bought a ticket on the Houston flight out of Dallas-Fort Worth 7.30 P.M. five days ago, but had failed to claim her seat. Beyond that there was nothing: nothing save an ugly sense of impending danger.

'Oh, Jesus!' Stoner covered his face with his hands. 'What the hell have we gotten into, Gerry?'

'I don't know,' Manners answered evenly. 'I know we're into something, but what is anyone's guess. We have to wait for Bob Ludlow to report in.'

Stoner nodded wearily. 'Yeah. You're right. But – hell, Gerry! – this is killing me.'

'Not yet.' Manners grinned tightly. 'So far you've been lucky.'

It was small consolation, and that evening Stoner found himself without appetite. He tried Fay's number several times up to midnight, but there was still no reply. He was unable to sleep, and for most of the night sat watching video tapes on the tv in his room. The next morning he appeared shaven, but haggard, and passed the day trying Fay's number or dozing as Bo and Luke turned cards and discussed the effects of the impending winter on the stock. Bo was of the opinion that the exceptionally fine summer meant an especially harsh winter, but Luke held that the good weather could hold through. Stoner made no attempt to join in, preferring to slump in silence, locked in his own private thoughts.

Five days later – days that, for Stoner, passed with hideously inexorable slowness – Ludlow called. Manners took it in his study, emerging to inform Stoner that the private investigator was coming over the next day around noon.

That gave Stoner something to hope for, and that night he slept better.

The next day Ludlow's dusty Lincoln came down the approach road like a welcome messenger. The detective climbed out looking several pounds lighter and pleased with himself. He wore the same crumpled brown suit, but it now seemed an even worse fit as he ambled over to the patio, where Stoner and Manners were waiting.

'What's this?' He ducked his head in the direction of Bo and Luke. 'You expecting something?'

Manners told him about Stoner's brush with the Chevy and the ensuing telephone call. Stoner told him about Fay.

'So they're on to you,' Ludlow murmured, fishing a cheroot from his breast pocket. 'Wonder if they've spotted me yet.'

He seemed unconcerned, and Stoner found that simultaneously reassuring and irritating. 'Did you get any-thing?' he asked.

Ludlow grinned, nodding. 'Yeah. I got a name. Like I told you before, that might not get us any farther, but I got some background, too.'

They sat down, falling silent as a servant poured them drinks, then Ludlow continued.

'The place is like you told me, Gerry. Only I guess you didn't notice the guys on the gate.'

Manners shook his head, and Stoner said: 'Rafe said they were heavies.'

'He was right,' Ludlow nodded. 'That place is sealed off like an Army research centre. Two men on permanent guard duty at the gate. Both armed. There's a patrol goes round the perimeter fence during the night – I couldn't get close enough to see if they carry weapons, but I'd guess they do. And the section Vereker uses – he lives inside, too – is sealed off even tighter.'

There was a pause as he flicked ash from his cheroot, then he took a folded sheet of paper from inside his coat and opened it with a dramatic flourish.

'I got inside, though. I couldn't risk staying too long, but I got what we wanted: a name. Thank God they don't use computer records – maybe Vereker's old-fashioned, but there's a nice little filing system there. Kept separate from the other files like they don't want the names getting out, but I guess that wouldn't be unusual. What I found was a cross-indexing system, so I used the names of the women to pin down the donor. You were right: they all got sperm from the same donor. And there's closer to one hundred and fifty than the thirteen you discovered, Mike.'

'Fourteen,' Stoner corrected. 'What's the name?'

'Grover,' Ludlow said. 'Colonel Vincent Conrad Grover. Lately of the United States Air Force, now some kind of high number with Lamont Pharmaceuticals.'

Manners said, 'I know that name. Wasn't he an astronaut?'

'Right.' Ludlow puffed smoke and for a moment the air was filled with an acrid smell. 'Grover was with NASA. He piloted the seventh and eighth shuttle landings. Then he got the command seat on the deep probe. Remember?'

The two men listening to him nodded. Stoner could remember the publicity that had attended the probe. For the eighteen months between official announcement and launching, a debate had raged on the wisdom and financial validity of the project. The pro side maintained that Deep Space One, as the programme was known, would give America a giant step ahead in the arms race; that it was another first for the country; that the expenditure was justified in terms of these advantages and the advanced technological gains to be made. The antis had argued that a country still suffering the effects of the world oil crisis could ill afford such luxuries; that the idea of using space as a weapons platform could only accelerate the shaky political situation; that NASA was a dead horse, and flogging it was just so much wasted effort.

Congress had been divided, and it had been the weight of Presidential support that shifted the balance in favour of Deep Space One. The probe had lifted at 8.00 A.M. on August 17th, two years ago. It had headed towards Venus, a mind-staggering 25,700,000 miles distant. There had been no intention of reaching the planet – not with a manned craft – but the three-man crew had gotten closer than any other human beings. They had been out for three months, and their return had come close to macabre fiasco.

Grover's companions on the probe had been another USAF man, a Lieutenant-Colonel Sangstrom; and a Navy man, Commander Talbot Fawcett. They had splashed down in the Pacific, and there had followed a sudden blanking of news coverage. Medical tests, the official announcement had said. When the tests were concluded and a curious public was granted a little more information, it was learnt that Arthur Sangstrom had lost his mind.

One year later – to the day – Fawcett had taken a .38 Colt Officers Model and spread his brains over the ceiling of a Tularosa motel room. Grover had seemed normal. He had given interviews, talking of the pressures affecting astronauts, the mental and physical stress of living for so long in a capsule little larger than a hotel bathroom. And the Deep Space project had been put quietly into mothballs. Grover had faded from sight, leaving NASA and resigning his USAF commission. He had been given an immediate appointment with Lamont Pharmaceuticals.

'And he was the donor?' Manners asked.

'The one and only,' said Ludlow, stubbing his cheroot. 'Real prolific.'

'That was all?' Stoner demanded.

'What more do you want?' Ludlow asked. 'There was medical stuff I guessed covered his sperm type, or something like that. But I couldn't risk taking a camera in there with me, and I wasn't waiting around to make notes. Grover was the donor, so I guess he's the next step.'

He sipped his drink, his ugly face thoughtful.

'That don't get us too far, does it?'

'Maybe.' Manners steepled his fingers, staring at his nails. 'Lamont headquarters are in Galveston. Suppose KXW decided to do a programme on him? Where do astronauts go after they've landed? That kind of thing.'

Stoner looked at him, waiting. Ludlow produced another cheroot and struck a match.

'I could set up a meeting,' Manners continued. 'At least get to see Grover. I could sound him out – maybe he'd listen. It'd sound authentic, at least.'

'It might work,' Ludlow allowed. 'You'd need to tread carefully.'

'I'm too well known,' Manners grinned with a confidence Stoner hoped he felt. 'Besides, I'd have people with me. I can fly down in the station's Lear. They – whoever the hell *they* are – wouldn't dare try anything. It'd be too public.'

'Maybe.' Ludlow didn't seem to share the television executive's assurance. 'But I'd like to come along. Just in case.'

'Where does that leave me?' asked Stoner.

'Here,' Ludlow said, his voice suddenly commanding. 'There might be word about Fay. And all of us going would be kinda like putting all our eggs in one basket.'

'You make it sound like they might get broken,' Stoner murmured.

'Yeah.' Ludlow's gaze was steady. 'They might. That's why you stay here.'

15

Two weeks passed before Manners was able to set up the meeting and he and Ludlow flew down to Galveston. Stoner waited in a fury of impatience for word. There was no news of Fay, and when he called her parents again, he found them equally confused and concerned. They had heard nothing from their daughter, and calls to the hospital elicited only the information that Miss Nicholas had taken a week's vacation – now passed – and had failed to report back for work.

Stoner found himself trapped in a limbo of frustration. He had no way of knowing whether Fay was dead or alive; and if she was still alive, where she was. The only place he could think of was the Walters Institute, though why she should be taken there, he hated to think about: there seemed only one possible reason. Fay was, after all, at an ideal age for bearing children; she was intelligent; she was healthy. The idea that she might have become forcibly involved in whatever was going on made the waiting that much harder; Stoner felt powerless as any of the sterile husbands.

Then, three days after Manners landed in Galveston, the television executive called the ranch.

'We saw him,' he told Stoner. 'He's a real credit to NASA and Dale Carnegie – a real Prince Charming. Told us all about the probe and what he's been doing since. Most of that's on record, so there wasn't much point in hiding anything. Sangstrom is in a nursing home in Colorado. Catatonic, by all accounts. Fawcett's suicide happened after his wife died. In childbirth!'

Stoner said, 'Christ!' very softly and waited for Manners to continue.

'Bob had his people check that out, and it sounds normal. Mother and baby died together – there was no evidence, at least according to records, of anything strange. Just an unfortunate accident. Grover puts the suicide down to that, coming on top of the probe.

'But when I mentioned the Institute, he clammed up. Said he knew nothing about it in a way that said he did. He told me he was happy to go ahead with a programme on ex-astronauts, but his private life was just that – private. I made a date for an in-depth interview, but when I called back to firm details, I got the old run-around. It appears that Grover has had to fly to Europe on urgent business. They can't say when he'll return, and they can't – or won't – give me a number to contact him. It's fishy, Mike. I've got a feeling we're getting close, and tracks are getting covered.'

'So what's our next move?' Stoner asked. 'I'm going crazy waiting, Gerry.'

'We're flying back today,' Manners replied. 'Hang in there, Mike. We'll be with you inside a few hours.'

'Yeah. OK.' Stoner put the 'phone down and got a beer from the ice-box. Bo and Luke were lounging on the patio, obviously bored with their guard duties. He stood by the window, watching them with the beer getting warm in his hand, then dropped into a chair and flicked on the tv. All the channels were showing dreck, offering him a choice between quiz shows, soaps, or B-feature westerns. He stood up, checking through Manners' library of tapes, and finally thumbed a recording of *She Wore A Yellow Ribbon* into the VCR, wondering how the persona Wayne had portrayed in so many movies would handle his situation. Ride on in, he decided, with one hand close to his gun. He chuckled cynically at his own musings and tried to concentrate on the tape.

Time passed. *She Wore A Yellow Ribbon* ended, and Stoner flicked the tv back to its normal programming. He fetched another beer and sat down to watch the news.

Abruptly, his attention was caught, riveted to the screen by a late item.

There was a long shot of smouldering wreckage strewn over a desert landscape. Smoke drifted from the jumble of tortured metal, most of it unrecognizable, only the high tailfin identifying the twisted chunks as an aircraft. The newsreader's voice, calm and impersonal, cut into his shock with knife-edge clarity.

'. . . earlier today. Amongst the victims were Dallas television executive Gerald Manners, Vice President of station KXW, and private investigator Robert Ludlow. The cause of the mid-air explosion is as yet unknown, but police and aviation authorities state that foul play is not suspected.'

Stoner thumbed the remote control, turning off the set. He was suddenly aware of sweat running cold and prickling down his back, and of a faint rattling sound. When he tore his eyes from the blank screen, he realized that the sound was his beer can drumming against the arm of the chair: his hands were shaking. He got to his feet, setting the can on a table as he crossed the room to pour himself a double measure of Jack Daniels. He downed the liquor in two fast swallows, then went to the 'phone, dialling the KXW number. Manners' secretary was tearful as she confirmed the news: Yes. Mr Manners was dead. The police had called. The jet had exploded in mid-air. There were no survivors.

Stoner went out onto the patio. He felt an odd calm descending, as though his options had been removed, leaving him without choice, with only one course of action. Whatever it was, it had to be better than merely sitting waiting.

Bo and Luke glanced at him and then both cowboys got to their feet, their tanned faces worried.

'Gerry is dead.' His voice was guttural. 'His 'plane blew up on the way back from Galveston.'

Luke said, 'Jesus Christ!'

Bo's mouth hung open, his eyes blankly uncomprehending.

'The Stingray.' Stoner gestured at the garage. 'Is it gassed up?'

Luke nodded. Then: 'What happened?'

Stoner said, 'I don't know. I think he was murdered. I'm going . . .' he decided against telling them his destination, '. . . away. The police may be round. If they ask you questions, say as little as you can about me. Tell them I took the car.'

Luke nodded, fingers stroking the butt of the Ruger Blackhawk as though he wanted to use the big pistol on someone.

'It's best you don't know any more than that,' Stoner said slowly.

'You think he was murdered?' Bo's voice was ugly with suppressed rage. 'Who done it?'

'I don't know,' Stoner said. 'I'm going to find out.'

Before either cowboy could question him further he went back inside the house. He dropped a change of clothing into a bag and added a Goushā road atlas. Then he went into Manners' study. There was a gunrack mounted on one wall, oiled weapons resting on pegs against the green felt background. Stoner fetched a Magnum down, the weight of the .357 Colt Python unfamiliar in his hand. God! he thought. I've not held a gun since 'Nam. Dully, he loaded the pistol, dropping extra shells into the pockets of his windbreaker before tucking the pistol in his holdall.

Luke had brought the Stingray out of the garage and the big engine was purring as though in anticipation. Stoner climbed behind the wheel with a feeling of finality, dropping the Colt on the passenger seat.

'You know how to use that?' Bo asked. 'It's got one helluva kick.'

'I know,' said Stoner. 'See you.'

He put the automobile in gear and tapped the gas pedal.

The Stingray surged smoothly forwards, leaving the two cowboys staring after it as Stoner accelerated down the approach road.

He had decided on a course of action now. More exactly, his options had been removed, leaving him with two simple choices: either wait for his own death at the hands of whatever ruthless organization was covering for the Walters Institute, or force a confrontation. He realized that a confrontation might well end in his own death, but he could see no other course open to him. He had had enough of waiting. Enough of nibbling around the edges of the thing, wondering who would die next. At least this way he was active, master of his own fate.

He went out of Dallas on US 287, heading northwest towards Wichita Falls and Amarillo.

It was dark by the time he reached Amarillo and he halted on the north side of town, booking into a motel. So far as he could tell, there was no pursuit, but at dawn the next day he checked the road map, deciding to keep to the secondary highways where there was less chance of his being spotted, or halted. He quit Amarillo on US 87, then followed US 129 to Raton, where he ignored the Interstate and cut off onto a two-lane blacktop that took him over to Alamosa. He drove all day, swallowing amphetamines when he felt tired, and by nightfall was in Pinedale, Wyoming. He halted there, eating a hurried meal before pushing on through the night, bolstered by the unnatural energy of the pills. By dawn he was in Idaho, starting to feel the disorientating effects of the amphetamines as he pulled into the parking lot of a motel off 191, just outside New Meadows.

He rose, feeling thick-headed, and breakfasted on black coffee and more pills. He followed 191 as far as Lewiston, then turned off to cross the Washington State line and cut back southwards into Oregon. He ignored Interstate 80, the toll road too easily checkable, and approached Portland on the secondary highways.

By now the amphetamines were taking a real toll, and he knew that if he continued his reserves of energy would be seriously depleted. He booked into a motel and slept for twelve hours.

Morning came clear and crisp and cold. The sky above the Cascades was an unbroken blue, and the half grain of Veronal he had taken before falling into bed had left him rested and fresh. There was a tang of salt in the air, coming in off the Pacific hidden beyond the bulk of the city. He breakfasted on ham and eggs, with waffles and a pot of coffee, as the Seeburg jukebox blasted Springsteen's latest hit across the diner.

The fury that had brought him to the city was dulled now, replaced by a sense of grim resolve that was underlaid with the beginnings of fear. In the clear northern light his self-imposed mission was suddenly daunting, and he realized that he had thought it through no farther than reaching the Institute. Now he was within a couple of hours' drive, and he was frightened. Rafe was dead. Manners and Ludlow were dead. Fay had disappeared. And Stoner was alone, facing some kind of organization that had made its intentions savagely clear. The answers he sought were, he was sure, locked inside the Walters Institute. But how the hell was he going to get inside? He could hardly drive up and ask for an appointment with Vereker, and Ludlow had said the place was patrolled by armed guards. It was a daunting proposition. But it was one he was determined to face.

And beat if he could.

He went out into the sunshine and climbed into the Stingray.

On the outskirts of the city, where Stark and 122nd Street joined, he found a clothing store, purchasing a thick plaid shirt and a lined windbreaker. He replaced his Keds with heavy-soled Dexters, changing in one of the

180

store's booths. He stuck the Magnum in the waistband of his jeans and zippered the windbreaker over the heavy butt. Then he left the Stingray in a long-stay park and went looking for a less distinctive vehicle. A Cherokee offered what seemed like a sound alternative, and he rented the four-wheel drive automobile for a week. Next, he bought a thermos and got it filled at a drive-in with black coffee that he laced with brandy.

It was now, he decided. Now or never: before his nerve went.

He started the Cherokee and drove north, following the directions given by Ludlow.

The road wound out of Portland, curving up into the mountains through steadily thickening stands of timber that covered the flanks of the hills like some sombre army, waiting; watching. Stoner drove to within a quarter mile of the Institute, where a blacktop cut away from the main highway, a sign stating that the secondary road led *To The Walters Institute Only*. He ignored the cut-off, following the highway on round the timbered slopes, climbing above the place until he was sure he was behind the complex of buildings. There he halted, taking the Cherokee off the road to wait for sundown.

The waiting was bad. It had been bad when he wasn't sure what he was waiting for; now – with the certainty that Fay was somewhere inside the place, and that death was a tool employed by the Institute – it was a whole lot worse. It reminded him of his tour in 'Nam: the times he had sat waiting for the big Bell-Hueys to lift off and drop him into a firefight. Then, at least, there had been others waiting with him, fellow medics or nervous grunts who shared his fear so that it became an accepted thing, something they could laugh at as the joints were passed around. Now he was alone. Not even sure what he was up against.

He was grateful for the setting of the sun – it ended the waiting.

He put the Cherokee into gear and shifted to the four-

181

wheel drive. Some kind of trail went down through the timber, heading in the direction he estimated the fence around the Institute lay. He followed it until it curved back in a southerly direction, then took off overland, hoping no one would hear the growl of the engine as he negotiated the rough country. He stopped when he saw lights filtering dimly through the trees and drank coffee. The night was cold and the hot, brandy-laced liquid served both to warm him and bolster his tensed nerves. A bright moon had risen, lending the forested slopes the aspect of a scene from a horror movie: the lone hero approaches the villain's lair. He paused in the shadow of a massive pine and checked the Magnum's load. The brass-jacketed cartridges glinted dully in the moonlight. Stoner wondered if he would need to use the pistol.

The slope steepened just beyond his position, running down in a grassy meadow to a shallow bowl banded on the far side by more trees. Stoner could see the lights glowing faint through the timber and guessed the fence must be somewhere on the far side of the pines. He slithered down the grass and ran across the bowl, waiting all the time for a shout of warning. Or maybe just a shot.

He reached the timber and ducked thankfully into the shadows, cursing as his feet crunched on the thick carpet of fallen needles. He moved cautiously forwards, the Magnum digging uncomfortably against his waist. A fold of land formed a kind of ledge here, the trees running out to the edge, then ending in a slight slope that was empty of cover. Stoner could see where stumps jutted from the ground, enormous trunks littering the gradient, beyond them the line of the fence. It could have been an honest lumber operation, but to Stoner's suspicious eyes, it looked more like a killing ground. He crouched in the darkness, staring at the fence.

Bulky metal posts supported a chainlink mesh around twelve feet high, an ominously thick strand of what looked like electric cable running along the top. Beyond, the ground was cleared, nothing but grass shining silvery in the moonlight for a space of around two hundred yards. Stoner moved on through the protective trees, looking for a place he could cross the fence.

Forty-some minutes later he found a likely spot. The ground dropped away into a small ravine, rocky-sided, with a stream gurgling down the centre. The naked stone ran under the fence, the gap too narrow to permit entry, but to one side, jutting from the slope, a gigantic pine thrust branches against the night sky. Several stuck out above the fence, tapering down to flimsy thinness where they crossed. Stoner took a deep breath and began to shinny up the bole. He reached a point where the branches jutted thick enough to afford him reasonably secure footing and began to ease out towards the fence. An owl hooted irritably as he disturbed its resting place and he felt sweat run cold along his spine as the ghostly shape launched itself from his approach. The branch swayed under him and he let go his hold on the higher limbs, easing down to a sitting position on the lower with his legs dangling either side of the wood. He began to work his way out, feeling the branch dip beneath him, praying it would not touch the fence to trigger some kind of alarm. He reached a point close to the fence and saw that if he went any farther, the tip would be forced down against the cable. Awkwardly, expecting at any moment to fall, he got his feet onto the limb and lurched upright, hands outthrust to grasp the branch above. His footing swayed precariously, but he succeeded in keeping hold of the higher branch, then began to swing himself along.

He shifted hand-over-hand, feeling the branch drag downwards so that he was forced to bend his knees, lifting his feet clear of the fence. Just short of the barrier he saw that any further forwards progress would dip the branch low enough that it would strike the chainlink. He hung there, knowing that he could not go back without risking the movement of his feet touching the cable.

And then, off to his left, he saw a light glimmer through the trees on the far side of the fence. It was a small light, the kind a handheld flashlight might make. The kind a guard might hold whilst making his rounds. Stoner took a deep breath and began to swing, curving his body in an arc that took his feet out over the fence.

He saw the light getting closer and let go his hold as his legs swung almost horizontal, fear pumping adrenalin through his body so that his metabolic rate speeded and his muscles seemed tireless. He let go the pine at the apex of his swing, curving out over the chainlink and the thicker cable to plummet through the air. He hit the grass on the far side feet first, rolling as though dropped from an incoming chopper. He felt his left shoulder strike the ground and let the movement continue so that he described a somersault, landing in a crouch two yards inside the perimeter. He flattened against the grass, twisting his head to watch the light as his right hand dug inside his windbreaker to find the butt of the Magnum.

He dragged the pistol out, coming up on his feet and running forwards as the light got brighter, emerging from the trees.

There was a stand of recently-planted conifers ahead of him and he hoped he could reach their cover before the guards spotted him. He was halfway over the distance when he saw that the light had been obscured by the moon and the shadows of the conifers. That it was a whole lot closer than he had thought. That the man holding the torch had a pistol of some kind holstered on his left hip. And that there was a second guard beside him, clutching a pump-action shotgun across his chest.

No longer obscured by the trees, the flashlight lanced brilliance through the night. Stoner saw the pool of light swing over the grass ahead of his position, then begin to swing slowly back towards him. He measured his length on the night-crisp grass, the Magnum gripped in both hands.

And light fell on his face as a voice cried, 'I see him! There!'

The light swung away, then back.

A second voice shouted, 'Hold it right there!'

And Stoner came up on his feet with the Magnum swinging to point at the blinding glow of the flashlight.

Adrenalin and the residual effects of the amphetamines transformed the scene to slow motion. Stoner could see the backwash of the torch illuminate the chest and the lower face of one guard. Saw the man fumble for the pistol on his waist as the other lifted the shotgun to his shoulder. For an instant that seemed to last forever, Stoner was looking directly at the ugly black hole of the shotgun's muzzle.

The guard said, 'He's got a gun!'

And Stoner saw the slight adjustment of his stance as he prepared to fire.

The Magnum bucked in his hand, the blast of sound taking him by surprise. Muzzle flash blinded him momentarily, and then he saw the shotgun tilt upwards as the guard flew back. His feet left the ground, arms flinging wide to hurl the shotgun away into the darkness. Stoner saw a brief spurt of blood erupt from the man's chest, and then he was racing for the safety of the conifers.

He was almost at the trees when he glimpsed a flash and heard the cough of a handgun. His left foot was smashed from under him and he pitched onto his face, feeling the Magnum fly loose as he. hit. He spat dirt, ignoring the stabbing pain in his ankle as he rolled towards the pistol.

He was almost touching it when the floodlight glared directly into his eyes and a voice, harsh with anger, said: 'Bastard!'

Then pain exploded inside his skull and there was only darkness.

16

A smell: sanitized, virtually odourless in its antiseptic anonymity. It was so familiar it took Stoner a while to identify it: the smell of a hospital. He opened his eyes and there was brightness. It came from the single fluorescent tube set at the centre of the white ceiling. He turned his head from the glare, recognizing the thick, muzzy feeling as the aftermath of sedation, and looked around. He was in a room as whitely antiseptic as the faint non-odour. There were no windows, just unadorned white walls, their blank uniformity broken only by the outline of a door, the stainless steel of the handle. He was in bed, a white sheet covering his body. He moved to sit up and found his limbs held still by retaining straps, another across his chest. They pinned him to the bed, not uncomfortable unless he tried to move, but inescapable.

He supposed he was lucky to be alive. Then wondered if that wasn't false consolation.

Craning his head up, he saw the smooth steel rails at the foot of the bed, a chart – its plastic back towards him – clipped to the topmost rail.

Then he gasped as a voice said, 'Welcome to the Walters Institute, Doctor Stoner.'

Craning his head back and round, he saw a surveillance camera mounted on the wall behind the bed, a small, mesh-covered microphone below it.

The voice said, 'Please be still. Someone will be with you.'

Stoner lay back on the low pillow, touching his tongue to lips that were dry. Whether from the effects of the sedatives he could sense in his body, or from fear, he was not sure. He swallowed, tasting sourness. The door opened and a man in hospital whites came in. The man was carrying a small plastic tray with a beaker and a hypodermic resting on a green paper napkin, he was short and bland-faced, thinning hair cropped tight against a round skull. He looked like any hospital orderly. He smiled, showing gapped teeth.

'You must be feeling a little logy.' A hinged table was pulled out from the wall to take the tray. 'We'll soon put that right.'

He peeled the sheet from Stoner's body and the doctor saw that he was naked, his left ankle encased in pressure bandages. The orderly – was he an orderly? – smiled sympathetically as he followed Stoner's gaze.

'You broke your ankle when you fell. A nice clean break, so there's nothing to worry about. Just keep your weight off that foot for a few weeks and you'll be right as rain.'

The banality of it frightened Stoner. He asked, 'The guard? Did I kill him?'

The orderly went on smiling without answering. Instead, he slid an arm under Stoner's shoulders and tilted him up enough that he could drink from the beaker. There was strength in the arm, more strength than the man's mild manner suggested. He held the beaker to Stoner's lips, positioning it so that Stoner was forced to drink. Then he dabbed antiseptic on the inner curve of Stoner's elbow and sank the hypodermic into the skin.

Still smiling, still terrifyingly normal, he picked up the tray and left the room.

Stoner stared at the door, feeling his eyes get heavy, feeling a sense of calm that was almost euphoric creep through him. He tried to hold his eyes open, but the tranquillizer was too powerful and he went down into an unwilling sleep.

When he woke again he was instantly aware of another presence in the room. He opened his eyes, feeling the retaining straps tug against his body.

'Don't try to move, you will feel a little groggy yet.'

The voice was soft, reassuring, faintly accented. There was a slight whirring sound and the speaker came into view. His face was only slightly higher than Stoner's, and the doctor saw that he was seated in a wheelchair, an electric motor powering the wheels, controls mounted on the wide arms. He was bald, his skull totally hairless, mottled with the purplish brown freckling that comes with age. His features, however, seemed ageless, caught at some point between vigorous manhood and eternity; there were no wrinkles on that face, no lines of laughter or displeasure or time. His eyes, shrouded by neither lashes nor brows, glittered black and piercing as a crow's. They shone with some kind of patina, drawing Stoner's gaze so that he blinked and looked away with conscious effort. His nose was large and romanesque, the skin smooth, folding down from the wide-spaced nostrils to a hairless upper lip thick as the lower, the mouth wide; smiling. His hands, Stoner saw, were as bland as his face, the nails pink and neatly trimmed, the fingers delicate. He was dressed in a black suit that emphasized the baby-like glow of his skin, the pants loose, seeming to fold in around legs too slender for the otherwise heavy body.

'I am Ivan Vereker,' he said. And Stoner felt his eyes drawn back to those moist, penetrating orbs. 'It is time we had a little talk.'

'Where's Fay?' Stoner heard his voice come out slurred, though his mind seemed to be working clearly. 'What have you done with her?'

'Miss Nicholas is in good health,' smiled Vereker. 'You might say she is blooming.'

'What have you done to her?' Stoner tried to resist the hypnotic power of those eyes.

'She is in good health,' Vereker repeated. 'In time – perhaps – you will be allowed to see her. To judge for yourself. That will depend on you, Doctor Stoner.'

Stoner frowned. 'What the hell are you talking about? Let me out of here or you're in trouble.'

It sounded feeble even as he said it, and Vereker chuckled, a curiously high-pitched sound.

'On the contrary, Doctor Stoner. It is you who are in trouble.' He raised a baby-soft hand to silence Stoner. 'Permit me to explain. Perhaps when you understand your position better you will adopt a different approach.'

'Go to hell!' Stoner snarled.

Vereker chuckled again.

'Hell, Doctor? A religious concept that has little to do with rational thought. Let us forget such abstract concepts as heaven and hell, and concentrate on our more immediate surroundings.'

The dark eyes seemed to glow, absorbing Stoner's defiance. Idly, he wondered if Vereker was a hypnotist: there was something both commanding and tranquillizing in that gaze – as though it could encompass all his fears, all his doubts, and offer a reassuring explanation. He watched the eyes, letting the words sink into his mind as might music, listened to in a darkened room.

'As I said,' Vereker continued, 'it is you who are in trouble. Let me summarize: you broke into a private establishment armed with a pistol stolen from Gerald Manners' home. You used that pistol to kill a guard. Oh yes, Doctor Stoner, the guard is dead. He was killed instantly – you are, it would seem, an excellent shot. That makes you a murderer, Doctor.'

'So hand me over to the law.' Stoner forced the words past the barrier of Vereker's gaze. 'I'll tell them everything.'

'It would achieve nothing,' smiled the bald man. 'Please let me finish. After all, your concern is for Miss Nicholas, is it not? And handing you over to face trial for murder would hardly aid her. Try to understand your position, Doctor. When I have explained, you can make up your mind.'

Stoner fell silent again, even his fear seeming to abate as Vereker stared at him.

'So, you are a murderer, Doctor Stoner. You came to Portland in a stolen car – you see, the fact that Gerald Manners is dead does not mitigate that relatively minor crime – and you came like a thief in the night. You have no real evidence to support what the local authorities would doubtless regard as a wild accusation against a highly respected citizen. Indeed, a citizen blessed with the full support of your own government. You were distraught. After all, several acquaintances had met with unfortunate accidents – accidents that seem to have unhinged you somewhat. At least to the point where your imaginings took over from rational thought. Mr Eddison will bear testimony to that effect. Did you not resign your position with the Dallas Memorial Hospital for that very reason?'

He chuckled again as a question formed on Stoner's face.

'Oh yes, Eddison has known for some time. His reports were most useful. As were those of Detective Rickenbacker. Perhaps I should put things in black and white for you: let you realize just what you are struggling against.

'Your movements have been monitored since your meeting with Laurence Anders. We had hoped that Eddison's warnings would persuade you to leave well alone, but it proved otherwise. You sent Antrim here, and that made it necessary to – well, we are speaking bluntly now – kill him. We had hoped that death would deter you, but you proved more obstinate than we thought. We tried to warn you off – it was Rickenbacker who drove that car the night you came so close to death. But even then you continued. Gerald Manners and the private investigator Ludlow became a nuisance, so it became necessary to remove them. The aircraft was a most opportune chance. It was felt by some to be a pity that you were not on board, but personally, I was pleased you escaped. You

190

have won my respect, Doctor. You are, after all, a most resourceful young man.

'We took Miss Nicholas as a further deterrent, though she has now proven to be the bait that ends this affair. You see, Doctor Stoner, this is the end for you. In one way or another.

'As things stand now, you are a criminal. A thief and a murderer. Should I hand you to the police, you would die before you came to trial. I can guarantee you that, just as I can guarantee that no questions would be asked. After all, who would either believe the rantings of a paranoid young man, or care much that he was shot whilst trying to escape arrest?

'In any event, doctor, we need waste no time discussing abstracts. You could die here and there would be no questions asked. An intruder is shot attempting to break in? Or a body is found in the hills? One more victim of these cold Oregon nights, lost in the mountains, his ankle broken.

'You are helpless, Doctor Stoner. You are alone and utterly helpless.'

He paused, as though allowing Stoner time for the words to sink in. The younger man lay beneath his retaining straps with the worm of fear growing afresh in his soul. It seemed a small worm, for Vereker's eyes continued to bore into his, denying his will to turn his head or close his eyes. Allowing him only the almost telepathic contact.

Finally Stoner asked, 'The government backs you?'

'I receive an appropriation,' nodded Vereker. 'Granted by Congress to aid the research I carry out. Beyond that, I receive further appropriations from an agency granted the right to operate independently.'

'The CIA?' Stoner muttered.

Vereker shook his head. 'The CIA knows very little of what I do, doctor. It is my opinion that the CIA is useless. An organization caught up in its own mystique, with sufficient fiascos on its records that it has become a laughing stock. Though it remains a useful scapegoat for more efficient departments. No, my funding – and the most useful help I receive – comes from another limb of government. I do not suppose you have heard of the IRS?'

'The Internal Revenue?' Stoner gaped.

Vereker laughed out loud now, higher pitched than his chuckle.

'Internal Research and Security, Doctor. The choice of initials was, I believe, deliberate. It serves to obscure the department's real activities.'

'Which are?' Stoner asked, the calm enforced by Vereker's hypnotic gaze allowing him a degree of genuine curiosity.

'In this instance, pure research.' Vereker touched a button on his chair and the apparatus moved closer to the bed. Stoner caught the faint whiff of peppermint on his breath. 'I am a geneticist, as you doubtless know. I developed my theories – had the chance to begin testing them – when that madman Hitler was attempting to establish his ridiculous Thousand Year Reich. You have heard of the concept of the *übermensch* – the superior man? I have that within my grasp, doctor. I am able to create a truly superior being.'

'Like Mengele?' Stoner grunted.

'Mengele?' Was anger showing on the bland face? 'That fool? A dotard, hiding in South America! A charlatan! Any fool can transform the colour of a man's eyes. No, doctor. Mengele played with bodies, taking enjoyment from suffering. I seek only the truth – the creation of superior beings. I seek to aid mankind on the next step of the evolutionary scale.'

'By killing women?'

'Unfortunately necessary.' Vereker's voice was calm; confident. 'Certain of your countrymen saw that when I was allowed into your country. The IRS sees it clearly. Yet how could we explain it to your great American public? Can you imagine the furore if it became known that genetic experiments were being carried out here? Do you think I could ask for volunteers? No, Doctor Stoner. I was forced to continue my research in secrecy, keeping my intentions even from those women accepting the sperm from my insemination banks.'

'Grover's sperm,' Stoner murmured.

'Not at first.' The moist, dark eyes became more intense. 'At first I used the seed of selected donors. There were prerequisites: physical condition, intelligence, an unsullied racial background. The result was a crop of exceedingly healthy children of high, though not abnormal, intelligence. I became what you might call a successful baby farmer.

'It was the research carried out by various other legitimate government establishments that afforded me the capabilities to achieve my goal. Nuclear research, Doctor. And the discovery of the DNA and RNA chains. Nature, you see, is slow. Evolution is a painful process. A step at a time; mistakes. Yet we develop faster than nature. Technological advances have outstripped natural development – witness your own country's destruction of the ecological chain – and if we are to avoid destroying this world in which we live, we must learn to control it better. To do that, we must become superior to the forces around us. It is our only chance.'

There was the sincerity of madness in his voice. Not mere fanaticism, but an even deeper conviction: a total belief.

'Grover afforded me the chance to achieve that aim. The Deep Space probe was the breakthrough I needed. I am not familiar with astronautical research, but I saw in Grover an ideal physical and mental specimen. The others were weak. Sangstrom, as you probably know, went mad. Fawcett took his own life when his wife died. But Grover was perfect. A widower with no ties, no allegiance beyond his desire to serve his country. He was superbly fit, his intelligence obviously high, his family history was impeccable. And yet, even then I did not suspect how valuable he would prove.

'You see, Doctor Stoner, the astronauts manning Deep Space One were subjected to particle bombardment across the entire spectrum. There is no point in confusing you with details, suffice it to say that Colonel Grover's reproductive system was altered – tests carried out on his sperm samples showed a change in the basic molecular structure. I saw that that change was the gateway I sought. I knew that Grover could be the father of a new race. A better race!'

He leant forwards in his wheelchair and Stoner saw a faint sheening of sweat on his unlined forehead.

'But how could I use that knowledge? The situation was delicate in the extreme. I could hardly ask for volunteers – apart from any other considerations, it was vital that the offspring enjoy a stable home background in order to reach a balanced maturity. And the answer was, as you Americans say, under my nose all the time. I saw that I had merely to accept the guests of my existing clinic. I had already established a most rigorous screening process: all I needed do was select a little more discreetly; choose the ideal recipients for Grover's sperm and inseminate them.'

'And kill them,' Stoner said quietly.

'Initially.'

Vereker nodded, easing back in his chair without shifting his gaze from Stoner's face.

'That aspect is inexplicable. Obviously something happens, resulting in spontaneous abortion. A foetal rejection so massive that the womb itself is destroyed; the mother with it. However, I believe I have now found the answer.'

Stoner waited, the worm growing now inside him, a deep, sick certainty forming in his mind.

'A controlled environment!' Excitement rendered

Vereker's voice guttural. 'Every aspect monitored to leave nothing to chance! Diet, exercise – all under my supervision. Here, where I can exercise total control. And you gave me that opportunity, Doctor Stoner. For that I am in your debt.'

The dark eyes seemed to grow, sapping Stoner's will as the full horror of it burst upon him. His voice was soft, hushed with awe and fear as he said:

'Fay.'

Vereker smiled hugely. 'Exactly! A healthy woman of perfect age. An IQ of 158. The perfect specimen, save for one thing.'

Stoner wanted to close his eyes, but found himself unable to make the effort. It was as though he lived a morning nightmare, horribly aware of the terror the dream induces, but not yet awake enough to end it.

'The background,' said Vereker. 'Do you see? If the child is to develop normally, he must have a family background. A father figure. You, Doctor Stoner!'

'He?' Stoner asked, not wanting to hear the answer.

'Of course,' Vereker chuckled. 'Miss Nicholas is pregnant.'

Now Stoner's eyes did close, though the nightmare continued. The threads were gathered. Neatly. Tied off. Like an umbilical cord. He wanted to vomit, but the drugs in his body wouldn't let him. He wanted to rise from the bed and put his hand on Vereker's throat, to feel his fingers sink deep into the smooth, yellowish flesh, to feel the cartilage crush under his grip and watch as the lunatic's eyes bulged. To kill the man.

But he was strapped securely to the bed. Held immobile, trapped as surely as a microbe on a slide.

'And it's a boy?' he asked hollowly, feeling hope drain from him.

'Yes.' Vereker's voice was calmly triumphant. 'Simple manipulation of the chromosomes ensures the foetus will be masculine.'

'And I'm to stand in as father figure?' His voice was harsh, despairing. 'I'm to become part of all this?'

'What other choice do you have?' Vereker said. 'Except, of course, to die. Do you want to die, Doctor Stoner?'

Slowly, so very, very slowly, the words torn from the depths of his torture, Stoner said, 'No. No, I don't.'

'Excellent!' Vereker's chair whirred as though applauding Stoner's decision. 'I felt you would see reason. You will need a little time to absorb what I have told you. To come to terms with it. But I assure you, Doctor Stoner, that you have made the right decision. You have chosen the path of life. You do humanity a great service, doctor. You and I and Miss Nicholas – we stand on the threshold of a new world. A better world, for my children will make it better.'

The wheelchair moved backwards, away from the bed. Stoner felt the power of those luminous eyes weaken, and he watched as Vereker rolled to the door and went through it as it was opened from the outside. It closed behind the geneticist and he was alone again in the white and silent room.

And then the silence was broken by a hoarse, rasping sound. Stoner realized it was the sound of his own weeping as tears coursed hot and heavy down his cheeks.

17

Autumn became winter. Snow covered the slopes of the Cascades, resting heavy on the dark branches of the pines, transforming the complex to Christmas card prettiness. Stoner stood, hands thrust deep inside the fur-lined pockets of his mackinaw, watching his breath steam on the crisp air. He could walk no farther in this direction for it would bring him to the cleared area around the fence and there a guard would turn him back. He could walk a quarter mile in any direction before a guard appeared, sometimes suspiciously unsmiling, sometimes casually friendly. Still guards, though. Still there to ensure Vereker's nuclear family would not stray from its appointed place. He turned around and began to trudge back through the calf-deep snow towards the cluster of buildings that formed the real centre of the Walters Institute.

The bungalow assigned him and Fay stood at one end of the low, pine-clad huddle that contained the laboratories and sperm banks. It was separated from the legitimate clinic by a double fence, reached by a narrow roadway that pierced the fence where two electronic gates barred the road. Two small huts stood either side of the double fence, each one manned at all times by two men, one to check – or turn away – visitors, the other controlling the gate. Stoner was confined as effectively as any prisoner of war.

His own quarters were comfortable, even luxurious, built on the lines of a skiing chalet. The bungalow was raised on stone piles, a wood porch running around two sides with a heavy storm door opening on a small vestibule so that entrance would not allow in the chilling mountain air. The vestibule opened on a large living area dominated by a huge stone fireplace. One wall was naked stone, the others – like the floor – polished pine. The furniture was Scandinavian, a mixture of wood, leather and chromed steel. Paintings by Klee and Renoir and Hockney hung on the walls, and they were all originals. There was a kitchen with a dining space off the living area, equipped with all the latest gadgetry. On the far side of the big room, a door opened on a corridor running out to the side of the building, giving access to a bedroom and a nursery, the bathroom, and an exercise room fitted out as a miniature gymnasium.

It was a whole lot more comfortable than the Nicholas's lodge in Aspen. And Stoner hated it.

He climbed onto the porch and went in the storm door, tugging off his mackinaw and snowboots to pad barefoot into the living area. Fay was curled in a gigantic armchair, clad in a cashmere sweater from Anne Klein and a heavy wool Halston skirt. She was reading a book, her tanned face glowing with health and the heat of the fire. She smiled as he entered.

'How is it outside?'

'Cold.' Stoner crossed to the kitchen and poured himself coffee: there was no alcohol permitted inside the bungalow. 'Cold and white and goddam lonely.'

'It's not so bad.' She set her book down, and Stoner saw that it was a current bestseller, some saga of the publishing industry by a man called Austin. 'At least we're together.'

He nodded, not feeling like arguing with her.

There had been enough arguing during the past months. At first he had put it down to the drugs they were fed: they seemed to have less effect on him than on Fay. They were getting tranquillizers of some kind – not too much, but sufficient that a mildly soporific mood was induced – and the regular dosage, combined with the sessions Vereker referred to as 'psychotherapeutic preparation' (and Stoner called 'brainwashing') had convinced Fay of the inevitability of programmed events. There were – of course – other considerations affecting her. The first few times Stoner had been allowed to meet her, hobbling awkwardly on a crutch, there had been anger beneath the dulling effects of the drugs. A sense of outrage at her kidnap and enforced insemination. But that outrage had waned as time passed and she accepted the fact of her pregnancy. The chemical changes occurring within her body combined with the drugs to create a sense of genuine motherhood, so that she had accepted their confinement more readily than Stoner, coming at last to an inner contentment. Even – he suspected – a sense of pride. He had made three escape attempts. Twice he had been turned back at the wire, and the last time the guards on the double gates had dragged him from the back of the garbage truck in which he was hiding. Now he, though to a lesser extent than Fay, had accepted the impossibility of escape.

He had contemplated inducing an abortion. Since his ankle had healed, they had been installed in the bungalow and granted a degree of privacy that had surprised Stoner until he realized there was no point to maintaining a close watch – there was simply nowhere for him to run. And he had thought of fouling Vereker's design with simple physical force. But he could not bring himself to hurt Fay. He was no longer sure that he loved her – her very acceptance of her fate seemed to emphasize the differences between them – but he could not bring himself to harm her, or the life growing inside her. So he waited, anticipating the moment the unnatural foetus began its spontaneous abortion. Vereker had assured them this would not occur. Three times weekly, Fay was examined, and Vereker delivered regular reports on her condition so that Stoner, despite himself, was involved by his own natural curiosity.

At some point – around the end of the year, Stoner thought – Vereker had become convinced they had accepted their fate. The drugs had ceased and Stoner was surprised to find himself ten pounds overweight, Fay a more modest seven. They had worked off the excess in the gym, and with long walks through the snowbound complex. Now they were both superbly fit, and the physical well-being Stoner felt served to emphasize the frustration of his confinement. At least until he saw that he was trapped as surely as Vereker had promised him he would be.

As Fay had said one night, a blizzard howling outside so that the luxurious bungalow with its roaring fire seemed a safe and secure place to be, almost homely, 'There's nothing we can do, Mike. I'm pregnant, and by the time the snow clears I'll be showing. We might as well sit back and enjoy it. Maybe it is like Vereker says – we're helping mankind.'

That, more than anything else, had convinced him of the hopelessness of escape, and he had allowed himself to sink into the routine of the days, even letting himself pretend that all *was* well.

He went over to the stereo system and put an old Dylan album on the Technics deck, one from the time before Dylan was born again. The compelling, nasal voice asked *Is your love in vain?* and Stoner sank onto the thick bearskin rug before the fire, stroking Fay's rounded calf with a gesture partly absentminded, partly sexual. She stroked his hair, her voice soft – or entreating? – as she murmured, 'It's not so bad, really.'

The snow melted and for a while the world was grey. Then fresh shoots began to push through the slush, daffodils and beds of crocus spreading patterns of brilliant colour over the winter-dead grass. The pines took on a healthy, verdant hue, and the sky got blue and clear.

Fay's stomach began to swell and Vereker's supervision became more intense. A ramp was constructed, running up to the porch so that the wheelchair was able to negotiate the rise, and the crippled geneticist became a frequent visitor to the bungalow. He continued to assure Stoner that all was going well, even promising that should there be any sign of rejection, he would personally supervise the abortion of the foetus before it could harm Fay.

Stoner found himself locked in a timeless limbo. The passage of the days meant little to him, for his life was circumscribed by the confines of the fences, and ahead of him there stretched the open-ended (or did he mean unending?) prospect of fatherhood: like a laboratory specimen with no life beyond the walls of the cage; no other reason for existence.

That in itself served to numb his mind, and he suspected that the drugs were being used again, introduced into his food or the water supply.

With nothing else to do, he allowed himself to become further involved in the experiment when Vereker suggested that, as a doctor, he use the facilities available to occupy his mind.

He took to visiting the laboratories and the extensive library, perusing everything he could find on genetic research and gynaecology. His knowledge increased, but the only concrete fact he was able to discover concerning Fay's particular case was that Vereker's experiment depended totally on the chance accident of Grover's mutated genes. Whatever hitherto-unknown form of radiation had bathed the astronaut during his months in deep space was a random factor, as uncontrollable as a wild gene – a kind of evolutionary outlaw, that might, or might not, produce the desired results. There was simply no way of telling.

Except the adoption of a wait-and-see attitude.

There was nothing else Stoner could do except wait and see; except, perhaps, to prepare himself as well as he was able to assist Fay in whatever way he could.

* * *

Spring blossomed and began to give way to summer. Fay's belly grew larger. And Stoner found himself torn between concern for her safety and an interest in the result. Fay herself seemed happy, even excited. She spent around thirty hours a week with Vereker, in sessions forbidden to Stoner and about which she would say little beyond that they were merely 'talkfests', the crippled geneticist assuring her of the value of his work. Stoner suspected that the man was using his almost-telepathic powers to convince her. Indeed, when Vereker spoke to him alone, he found the compulsion of those shining black eyes too powerful to resist, felt them sap his will so that he, too, was convinced of the man's sincerity.

The difference was that the hypnotic effect wore off after a spell, while in Fay's case it seemed permanent.

She continued to swell, bouts of morning sickness alarming Stoner until Vereker allowed him to attend a check-up session and he was forced to admit that she appeared perfectly normal.

Twice during the spring, once in mid-February then again in March, Fay suffered acute stomach cramps. On both occasions Stoner used the telephone to alert Vereker, who appeared at the bungalow with two doctors and a grey-haired, stone-faced nurse, to administer pills and carry out a detailed examination. The cramps passed as swiftly as they had come, and Stoner began to let himself believe in Vereker's assurances that the confinement was going exactly as planned.

And spring became summer, the hills lush with foliage. Fay took to studying fashion magazines and catalogues of babywear, beginning to plan for the birth like any normal, expectant mother. She supervised the redecoration of the nursery, changing the colour scheme three times, obviously delighting in the freedom of Vereker's no-expenses-spared attitude.

Stoner took to smoking a pipe he scrounged from a guard. Until Vereker – almost apologetically – suggested that even the herbal tobacco he was using disturbed the controlled environment. Stoner gave up the pipe and settled into the role of nervous father-to-be.

And Fay went on getting bigger.

It was July, towards the end of the month. The night air was warm and the bedroom windows were opened, screened against mosquitoes. The sky was clear, a deep velvet blue that was brilliant with stars and the light of the near-full moon. Stoner lay awake, watching Fay's sleeping face. She looked lovely, perhaps more beautiful than he had ever seen her. Pregnancy had given her a bloom that was further enhanced by the pure mountain air and the carefully-controlled diet. Moon's light filtered through the screens, emphasizing the clean, statuesque planes of her features. Her blonde hair was loose on the pillow, grown out to shoulder length and bleached a pure gold by the sun. One slender arm was outside the sheets, her hand resting on the lower edge of the swell that bulged her stomach, a slight smile curving her full lips.

In that moment Stoner knew that he loved her. Not the way he had loved her before, but perhaps in a deeper, more lasting manner. He wasn't sure, nor did he wish to analyse it: it was something that was simply there, unquestionable. He wondered how things might have turned out had he never wondered about Marianne Anders, never discussed his fears with Rafe Antrim; had been turned away by Gerry Manners.

None of that seemed to matter in that moonlit moment.

He was here. Now. Watching the woman he loved.

It didn't even matter that she was fertile with the sperm of another man.

She was pregnant.

She was soon to bring a child into the world, and the circumstances of that birth no longer seemed important.

He reached out a hand, resting it lightly on the swell of her belly.

And he felt movement.

Against his palm he could feel the motion of the child, as though it kicked the confining walls of the womb, eager to emerge.

And Fay's eyes opened. Wide, a faint groan escaping her lips.

She said – very calmly – her voice clear and confident, 'Mike! I think he's coming.'

Stoner leapt naked from the bed, left hand flicking on the light switch as his right grabbed the telephone. The connection was instant, the voice at the other end unblurred by sleep.

He said, 'She's started.'

The voice replied, 'We'll be over.'

The 'phone went dead.

Stoner felt Fay's hand clutch his arm as a spasm racked her and he said, 'Fay, I love you.'

'I love you.' Her voice was suddenly harsh with pain. 'It'll be all right. Won't it?'

He nodded and began to tug on jeans and a sweatshirt.

He was lacing his sneakers when the outer door opened and he heard the whine of Vereker's wheelchair. The bald-headed geneticist rolled into the bedroom without preamble, followed closely by the stone-faced nurse and two bulky men in white tunics carrying a stretcher trolley. With impersonal efficiency they peeled the sheets from the bed and lifted Fay onto the stretcher. Vereker said, 'Hurry. Come with us, doctor.' Stoner nodded, clutching Fay's hand as she was carried out to the living area. The stretcher was trundled into a clear plastic tent that sealed over Fay's body, one of the white-tunicked men connecting an oxygen bottle to an inlet point close by her head.

Stoner said, 'It'll be all right, Fay. I promise you.'

The men carried the stretcher smoothly out of the bungalow and Stoner followed Vereker's buzzing wheelchair the short distance to the delivery room.

The place was sealed off behind air-tight doors, fluorescents gleaming brilliantly from the ceiling as Fay was eased into the chair, her feet secured in the stirrups. Vereker motioned Stoner into an observation cubicle, his lineless face animated for the first time Stoner could remember.

'I have one regret,' he murmured, and Stoner noticed that his voice was guttural with excitement. 'That I am unable to deliver this child myself. But you, Michael? Would you not like to attend at the birth of a new era?'

Stoner nodded, and Vereker pointed to a door.

'Get scrubbed, then. Hurry.'

Stoner went through the door and found himself in a preparation room. He stripped, stepping hurriedly beneath the shower, soaping himself vigorously before climbing into the drying cubicle. A male nurse appeared with a sealed package of clothes and Stoner dressed in the dull green garments, not thinking about anything except the need to help Fay. Doubts were forgotten now, replaced by the more urgent need to be with – to comfort and help – the woman he loved.

He went out of the dressing room into a sterile corridor. The nurse pointed at a door and he went through, finding himself in the delivery room.

Sweat was sheening Fay's face, her hair drawn back beneath a skullcap, so that the contortion of her features was emphasized. She saw him approach and wailed, 'Mike! Help me, Mike! Oh, God! He hurts. He hurts me, Mike!'

Stoner took her hand. The palm was moist, her fingers fierce and clutching and frightened as she gripped him. He could feel her body trembling, straining to deliver . . . *what?* Suddenly he felt fear knot cold in his belly. He answered the pressure of Fay's demanding fingers with an intensity of his own. Beneath his surgical mask he felt the breath come in gasps, irregular.

And the question drummed in his mind: *What?*

What would emerge from Fay's womb?

He stared as fluid burst from between her widespread legs, wincing as she screamed, feeling sweat cold on his face.

He saw something bloody emerge, then lost sight as the attendant doctors blocked his view. Fay screamed afresh, a wailing, throat-wrenching howl of pure agony. And then the sound tailed off to a whimper, the pressure of her grip easing slightly.

The doctors stepped back and Stoner saw one of them lift a bundle wrapped in a caul of bluish-grey membrane as another severed the umbilical cord, a third clearing the caul. Through the glass of the observation room, Stoner could see Vereker's face, the dark, moist eyes wide, glittering with excitement, with anticipation, as he peered eagerly at the child.

The geneticist's voice, tense with barely-suppressed eagerness, came over the intercom: 'He lives?'

At the same time Fay asked, 'Is he all right?'

The doctor holding the child began to turn, moving towards Fay. Stoner saw a baby, tiny, wrinkled organs attesting to his maleness, the head large with a pronounced cranial cavity, the skull thick with dark, damp hair, the limbs normal, well-shaped. The child was silent, though his eyes were open, seeming to scan the room with a penetrating blue gaze.

Stoner opened his mouth to say, 'Yes. He's fine.'

But a voice that was not a voice dinned in his mind as the blue-eyed gaze fastened on Fay's breasts.

It said, 'I am.'

Then, louder: 'I AM.'

Stoner stepped towards the infant, his mouth gaping open, but something froze his limbs, pushing him back as the silent, wordless voice roared through the delivery room and a nurse began to scream as forceps and pincers and kidney bowls scattered noisily over the floor, the clatter of their falling drowned beneath that wash of non-sound: demanding, eager, triumphant.

I AM.

Stoner stared at the child and through his mind, like a newsreel shown in fast motion, there flickered images of Rafe Antrim, of Gerald Manners, of Bob Ludlow; knowledge of the dead women; a vision of the burning aircraft; a memory of the Chevy trying to drive him off the road.

And there was triumphant dismissal that pushed those thoughts from his mind as the voice that was not a voice repeated, even as he formed the words *Oh my God*:

I AM!